PLAYGROUND

50 CENT

with

LAURA MOSER

Illustrations by Lizzi Akana

razor
bill

An Imprint of
Penguin Group (USA) Inc.

Playground

RAZORBILL

Published by the Penguin Group
Penguin Young Readers Group
345 Hudson Street, New York, New York 10014, U.S.A.
Penguin Group (USA) Inc., 375 Hudson Street, New York, New York 10014, U.S.A.
Penguin Group (Canada), 90 Eglinton Avenue East, Suite 700, Toronto, Ontario, Canada M4P
2Y3 (a division of Pearson Penguin Canada Inc.)
Penguin Books Ltd, 80 Strand, London WC2R 0RL, England
Penguin Ireland, 25 St Stephen's Green, Dublin 2, Ireland (a division of Penguin Books Ltd)
Penguin Group (Australia), 250 Camberwell Road, Camberwell, Victoria 3124, Australia (a divi-
sion of Pearson Australia Group Pty Ltd)
Penguin Books India Pvt Ltd, 11 Community Centre, Panchsheel Park,
New Delhi – 110 017, India
Penguin Group (NZ), 67 Apollo Drive, Mairangi Bay, Auckland 1311, New Zealand
(a division of Pearson New Zealand Ltd)
Penguin Books (South Africa) (Pty) Ltd, 24 Sturdee Avenue, Rosebank,
Johannesburg 2196, South Africa

Penguin Books Ltd, Registered Offices: 80 Strand, London WC2R 0RL, England

10 9 8 7 6 5 4 3 2 1

ISBN 978-1-59514-434-8

Library of Congress Cataloging-in-Publication Data is available

Printed in the United States of America

Introduction

I'll be the first to admit that not everything I've done in my life has been role-model material. I've been on the wrong side of the law. I've been in violent situations. I've also been a bully. I know how a person gets to be like that. That's why I wanted to tell this story: to show a kid who has become a bully—how and why that happened, and whether or not he can move past it.

Writing *Playground* was a personal journey for me. There's a lot of me in Butterball. I drew on events that happened in my childhood and adolescence as well as things I saw around me. I also tapped into some of the feelings I remember having at that age—feelings about my family, feelings about my future, feelings about other kids on the playground.

Living life on the edge has taught me a lot, like the fact that being mentally strong will get you ahead in life. But being a bully won't get you anywhere. Some kids don't figure that out until it's too late. Does Butterball? You'll have to read the book to find out.

Curtis "50 Cent" Jackson III
New York, New York

"Don't call me that."

"I'm sorry, I don't understand." She shifted in her seat, and I looked around the room again. I couldn't believe how depressing her office was. It was a small room on the second floor of a strip mall, above a dry cleaner's, and one storefront over from a Popeyes. The whole place stank like week-old fried chicken, and I was supposed to take this skinny white woman seriously?

"Listen, lady, I'm sure you mean well, but let's you and me get one thing straight right now. I'm here because if I get expelled from school, I'll have to sit around my mom's apartment all day, and if I have to sit around my mom's apartment all day, I'll go even crazier than I am already, know what I'm saying? So I'll sit here with you, but only if you ease off."

"That's perfectly all right, Bur—"

"What, are you deaf or something? Didn't you hear me say don't call me that like ten times already? I go by Butterball, all right? Bu-tter-ball," I sounded it out. "It's not that hard."

The woman nodded, tugging at a few strands that had come loose from her bun. It was impossible to tell how old she was. She could be thirty-five or fifty-five; I really had no clue. "All right then. Do you mind if I ask how you feel about being called Butterball?"

"How do I *feel*?" I laughed. "C'mon, lady, this has to be a joke. How long am I supposed to sit here again? Is it forty-five minutes or an hour?"

She pursed her lips together tightly. "Our sessions run forty-five minutes, or as long as I feel is appropriate. And for the record, I don't answer to 'lady.' You can call me Liz or Ms. Jenner, whichever you like, but those are your only options."

I laughed again. This woman was really cracking me up. "Liz? Yeah, no, thanks, but no thanks."

"Ahem—*Butterball*. However you want to play this is fine with me. I'm perfectly happy to go at your pace."

"Great."

"All right then."

She folded her arms in front of her and sat very still, staring right at me without speaking. I fixed my eyes on the ugly painting of three sailboats under a smeary blue sky that was hanging right above her head. What kind of fool would choose a picture like that? It had no detail, no point of view, no nothing—like a piece of art chosen as a movie prop to show the character in question has zero taste.

From downstairs, the fried-chicken smell kept getting stronger and stronger. And don't think I didn't see the way that therapist was staring at me—like she'd better lock up her valuables when I'm around, not that this shitty office had anything worth half as much as my pair of sneakers.

I'm not sure how many minutes passed—three, five, ten? But it looked like this white lady wasn't going to budge. Seemed like she might have even been as stubborn as my mom, and that was saying something. She just kept on sitting there staring at me, until finally I had no choice but to say, "All right, fine. You can ask me questions, but I don't have to answer them. How's that for a deal?" *You crazy bitch*, I was too polite to add.

"Well, I guess that's fine, then. I appreciate that. Let's just start with the basics, Butterball, shall we?"

I snorted. "Sure, we *shall*."

She ignored me. "How about we start with your telling me when exactly you moved to Garden City?"

"That's as good as you got?" I sneered at her, but I was relieved as all hell that she still hadn't mentioned the reason I'd been dragged to her office that day. Because if there was one thing I would never, ever discuss with this uptight white woman, it was Maurice. Not in a million years.

I know Liz had already conferred with the school principal and my mom and all that shit, and I'm sure she'd read the report about why I'd been sent to her. And she'd probably gasped out loud when she got to the part about how I popped Maurice on the playground last Friday. Tight-assed lady like Liz, I wonder what she would've said if I'd told her all the parts the report left out, like how I'd woken up that morning and pulled that special sock out of my underwear drawer and filled it, one after the other, with the D batteries I'd bought at Duane Reade the last time I visited my dad in the city. But there was no way. There was just no way I'd ever

tell Liz or anyone else what really went down that day, or what my reasons for it were.

When I got to school that morning, I felt ready for anything, like Bruce Lee, James Coburn, and Kareem Abdul-Jabbar all rolled into one large-ass pair of pants. The morning dragged on like it always did, but that day I had no trouble staying awake in geometry or social studies. I was pumped. I knew what I had to do, and I couldn't wait to do it. Not to get it over with, but to savor every last second of it. My sweet revenge.

At lunch I was too hopped up to eat, and anyone who knows me understands how janky that was. But no one noticed because no one at J. Watkins Junior High School gave a shit about my fat ass one way or another. That was about to change; I was sure of it.

After lunch the playground was more crowded than usual, and that suited my purposes fine. "Hey, Maurice!" I called out when I saw him sitting on the bench by the monkey bars. He was alone and had a book open in front of him, but that was pretty much how it went with Maurice. He had zero friends—why would he?—and spent all his free time reading.

When I said his name, Maurice looked up at me with a funny expression, almost like he knew what was about to happen. But I play fair, so I gave him a chance to defend himself. "Hey, Maurice, I think it's time you learned what happens when you talk shit about me," I said.

"What do you mean, man?" he asked with what might or might not have been a smile. It was always hard to figure out what Maurice was thinking, whether he was making fun of me or not. Well, he was about to stop laughing.

"Hey, Maurice," I said again, and this time I was shouting, walking toward him a little faster. My right hand was in my sweatshirt pocket, all five fingers clenched around the heavy sock that was going to teach Maurice who was in charge from now on. "There's only one way I can think of to keep your mouth shut, and that's to shut it myself."

Maurice rose from the bench, and now his expression was definitely frightened. He put down his book and took a few steps toward me, and that's when I gave it to him. I reached into my pocket and *BAM!* I whacked Maurice right across that self-satisfied grin of his, and I pounded those batteries into his teeth over and over until I felt something come loose.

I heard the sounds around me, the gasps and the cheers and the screams, but in that moment there were only two people in the entire universe, and that was me and Maurice.

Maybe the report on Liz's desk covered the highlights

of how I'd barely even gotten started when Maurice collapsed onto the asphalt with both hands clasped over his mouth, and how the blood flew everywhere until it seemed to be coming out of his ears.

But no stupid-ass guidance-counselor write-up could possibly have described how *good* it felt, taking out the sock I'd stashed in my backpack and slamming it hard against his face. *Take that, Maurice. That'll show you not to mess with me again, not to spread around lies like they weren't nothing.*

When I pulled my hand away from his face for the last time, I suddenly became aware of how the whole scene had gone completely silent all around us: how all of those kids just stood there staring at me like I was finally something. And I'd be lying if I said that didn't feel pretty damn good.

Annoying old Liz was still running through the most boring questions like I was applying for a job or something. But I was okay with that because as long as she stuck to the small stuff, the minutes would keep flying by. Besides, I kind of liked getting to talk without someone always interrupting me. Ever since my mom and dad split up, it seemed like no one ever had time to listen to anything I had to say.

"So, tell me, Butterball—do you have any friends at school?"

I glared at her. What kind of question was that, anyway? "Yeah, I've got friends. Why wouldn't I have friends?"

"Sorry, I phrased that wrong," Liz said, flashing her yellow teeth at me. "Of course you have friends. What I wanted to know was—well, do you care to tell me about them?"

"Not really," I said, and when I saw that didn't satisfy Liz, I went on, "They're just guys. No one special. All the black kids at Watkins kind of stick together, mostly because we don't have much choice in the matter, know what I mean?" I looked over at pale pasty Liz and thought, *No, of course she didn't.* "Most of my real friends are in the city, but I only get to see them on the weekends I visit my dad. My boys in school here, I mean, we just hang out during the day, you know—we don't see each other on the weekends much."

Liz nodded and jotted something down in her cheapo spiral notebook. "So has it been difficult for you, leaving your old friends behind and moving to a new school?"

"Nah, why would it be? Like I said, I got plenty of friends here, and besides, I still go to the city all the time. If I didn't, yeah, times might be a little tougher out here in Garden City."

Another curt nod from Liz. "What about girls? Do you have any . . . romantic interests?"

I snorted my drink through my nose at this. "Oh,

man, you really have a funny way of putting stuff, do you know that? No, I don't have any 'romantic interests.'"

"All right, then, that's fine. And what about—"

"I mean, there's this one girl who's a friend of mine. Her name's Nia, and she's really nice to me. Well, not to me exactly. She's just a nice girl, you know? To everyone. And she's having a party in two weeks that I'm going to. It should be pretty tight."

Liz looked pretty interested in this little tidbit. "So you're looking forward to that, then?"

"Isn't that what I just said?" Irritated, I shook my head and looked down at my feet. My Nike X Series had been the coolest shoes ever when I got them almost two years ago, right when my parents split up and were feeling guilty about shit. My feet had grown some since then, but I didn't care. My feet hardly blistered any-more, and even if those shoes had seen better days, they still looked pretty hot. Yeah, some of the leather had faded on the sides, but nothing a little coloring in with a Sharpie couldn't fix.

Still, I knew I needed to make a splash at Nia's party the weekend after next. That is, if she ever got around to inviting me. Before, I'd been pretty sure it would happen, since Nia had always been so friendly with me and all. But I hadn't been back to school since the whole deal went down at the playground, and I wasn't sure what she thought of me now. Maybe if she hadn't been there, if I hadn't caught her eye right as I walked over to Maurice . . .

Nah, but it didn't do any good to think that way. Still, I couldn't stop picturing, like a shot in slow motion, the look on her face after Coach Reese tackled me and led me back into the building with my arms pinned behind my back like I was a drug dealer or something. Nia was standing there with her mouth hanging open, and she looked scared to death—of *me*.

I heard a sound in the outer lobby. "Yo, I think it's time for me to take off. My mom's working tonight, so she doesn't have time to sit around waiting for me." I rocked out of my seat; I couldn't wait to get out of that crazy fried-chicken-smelling cave.

"All right, Butterball. I've really enjoyed talking to you today, and I look forward to our next meeting. I think the two of us can make a lot of progress together, I really do."

"Yeah, whatever." And I was out of there.

Liz told my mom she needed to see me at least twice a week at first, or until she could "detect real improvement," whatever that meant.

I hadn't missed the flustered expression that crossed Mom's face when Liz broke this news to her. I could see the dollars and cents signs flashing. Not for the first time, I wondered, but wasn't about to ask, how much cash my mom was coughing up for these little sessions with Liz. But I figured that was my mom's problem for now. Talking it out with a loser social worker in a strip mall was a whole lot cheaper that sending me to a private school as Principal James had first suggested.

Going anywhere other than Watkins was never gonna be an option.

Our next appointment took place the following Monday, right after my first day back at Watkins.

"What was it like, being back in school?" she said before I'd even really gotten to take off my backpack and open my PowerQuench. I like to settle into things, kick my feet up, but that wasn't Liz's style.

"It was . . . pretty good, actually," I said, and I was telling the truth. Though Nia had kept her distance, a bunch of other guys had actually been nice to me for the first time ever. Like they finally respected me.

Liz looked down at her notebook as she asked, "Was Maurice back in school today?"

It was the first time she'd ever mentioned my enemy by name, and I met her stare easily, then shrugged. "Yeah, I think so, but I didn't actually see him. He got transferred out of my math class, and that's the only time we ever crossed paths anyway. Watkins is a real big school, you know. There are like seven hundred people in each grade."

"So that's a positive development," Liz said. "The fact that Maurice is already back in school."

"If you say so," I said with another shrug. And then,

when Liz resumed her psycho staring, I added, "But you gotta understand, that nerd would rather take a bullet than miss his precious classes. I'm sure anyone else would stay home longer—you know, take advantage of the situation to kick back a little—but not Maurice." I laughed, thinking about what a loser he was. "My boy Bobbie, he saw him in social studies and said he looked plenty messed up. But apparently there was nothing really wrong when they checked him out at the hospital. Just a split lip, but no loose teeth or nothing like that. I don't think he even needed stitches on his lip."

That's why his nice rich parents decided not to press charges—because no real damage had been done.

"Who's Bobbie?" Liz asked, surprising me. It wasn't the follow-up question I'd expected. "Can you tell me about him?"

"Bobbie's just this guy at school," I said. "He's cool."

"I see," Liz said, scribbling something in her notebook.

Bobbie was second in command of Andres's posse, a kickass basketball player who was about seven feet tall and ripped and could date any girl he wanted, including at the high school. He'd high-fived me in the cafeteria that morning when I'd gone in for my chocolate milk and said I should check out Maurice's busted-up face. Bobbie's the one who told me Maurice was planning to eat in the nurse's office from then on.

"Anything else happen today?" Liz had stopped writing and was staring at me again.

I shook my head. "Nah, it was just the same old shit as always."

Except that at lunch Andres had high-fived me, too, and so had Darrell, and they'd even told me I should come sit with them. But by the time I had made it out of the hot-food line with my tray, their table was already full, so instead I just waved and kept on walking to my usual table in the back corner by the recycling bins no one ever used. I was pissed to see that, during my week on suspension, two geeky-ass seventh-graders had tried to edge in on my domain.

"Get the hell out of here, you assholes," I said, slamming my tray down right on top of the littler kid's— I'm pretty sure his name was Jamal—Fried Fish Delight. After the two kids scurried away without even taking their food with them, I had the table all to myself again, and that was just how I liked it.

• • •

"So there's nothing else you want to tell me about?"

She was really persistent, this Liz. But I didn't crack that easy and kept on just shaking my head. I didn't think she cared to hear about how I actually kind of liked the way people, even teachers, looked at me differently in the halls all day long, like I was someone worthy of respect, not just another big invisible blob.

My second appointment with Liz went by faster than the first one, and by the time I walked out of there, I wasn't even in all that bad a mood. Old Liz was all right in her way. She may not be all that smart, but at least she could sit there and listen without interrupting all the time.

Outside it was rainy and cold, a deep gloominess that never seemed to fall over the city, or that all the big buildings did a good job of concealing. I saw my mom's old Honda and jogged over toward it. I'd already opened the passenger door before I noticed that the person behind the wheel wasn't my mom but her friend Evelyn. I hesitated, but just for a second, before sliding into the seat. I don't know why I was even surprised anymore.

"Where's my mom?" I asked, looking straight ahead

of me. "Because I don't need a babysitter anymore, you know."

Evelyn sighed and shook her head. "Apparently you do," she murmured, as if I couldn't hear her. She only pretended to be nice when my mom was around. When it was just the two of us, the gloves came off. In a louder voice she said, "Your mom is working the night shift, as I believe she told you this morning."

"Yeah, yeah, right, of course she did." My mom had missed a ton of shifts during my suspension, and she hadn't let me forget it. "It's just I thought the night shift didn't start till the night, and last time I checked it was like five o'clock in the afternoon. But whatever."

Evelyn just sighed: her specialty. But then, after a pause, she asked, "Do you have any makeup work I can help you with? Your mom thought maybe you'd have a lot of assignments after a whole week away."

"I can do my own damn assignments," I snapped. "I don't need any help from you."

"All right, then," Evelyn said in her sad old-lady way. "I was just offering."

We drove the rest of the way in silence, and when we got home, Evelyn immediately switched on the TV and went into the kitchen to start dinner. She didn't say anything else to me, so I just sat on the couch waiting for the right time to make my escape. I was hungry, and Evelyn never made me food I liked, and she always kept the TV on stupid true-crime shows that sucked, and she didn't even watch them because she was in the next room making beans and tofu (I'm not joking) and all sorts of other nasty crap no one in his right mind would eat.

After a few minutes, Evelyn came in and placed a bowl in front of me. "Veggie chili," she said. "Try it." Instead of looking at me, she started tidying the room, arranging our shoes in the corner and stacking up the books I'd dumped out of my backpack.

"I ain't hungry," I said and shoved the bowl away. That wasn't true. I was starving, but I wasn't going to give Evelyn the pleasure of eating that disgusting sludge she'd put in front of me.

She didn't seem to care either way. "Suit yourself,"

she said. And then she stood up, switched off the TV, and walked into my mom's room with a book. Well, if she didn't like me hanging around her, I'd give her her precious space. Evelyn and I were pretty much through with pretending around each other.

I fished around my backpack for some money and dug out two quarters and three dimes, just enough for a Snickers bar. I spread my books out across the little table again, then grabbed my portable video camera, the Panasonic I'd bought when my old flip cam got jacked on the subway, just in case I ran across anything cool to shoot. Yeah, right. There was never anything worth filming in ugly Garden City. No street life, no action at all.

"I'm going outside," I said after a few more minutes of silence. Evelyn didn't respond, not even to remind me of my mom's favorite subject, which was that I was grounded for life. Well, screw her, too. I pounded down the steps and out the front door.

On the stoop was a little kid, Malik, who was maybe eight or nine and lived in the basement apartment with his mom and grandparents.

"Get outta my way," I said and shoved him off his perch.

He fell flat on his ass on the top step and burst into tears. Whatever, I'd done him a favor. Stupid little kid like that shouldn't be on the street at this time of night, not even in Garden City. He was lucky I didn't do a lot worse to him. It'd teach him a lesson.

"Yeah, of course I love my dad" I said. I'd only been there five minutes and already Liz was starting in again. "Why wouldn't I? He's the bomb. We'd still be living with him—and be a lot happier, too—if my mom hadn't walked out on him like she did. It wasn't *his* fault she left," I added, in case that wasn't totally clear already. Sometimes you had to spell shit out for old Liz.

Liz leaned forward, nodding in that annoying way she had. "And can you tell me why you think your mom, as you put it, walked out on him?"

I shrugged. I couldn't believe Liz actually got paid to just sit on her ass and repeat everything I said right back to me. Then again, I thought, looking around the dark little fried-chicken room, she clearly didn't get paid *that* much. Yeah, my mom could definitely afford Liz on the kind of overtime she worked.

"Damned if I know," I said finally, when she just kept on staring at me. "My mom's just one of those types who's never satisfied with what she's got, you know? Nothing's ever good enough for her—not her job and definitely not my dad's. But it wasn't his fault he couldn't live up to some nonexistent standard of perfection she set up in her brain, was it?"

"So your dad," Liz said, "he wanted your mom to stay?"

"Hell, yes, he wanted her to stay—haven't you been listening? For that whole first year, he was practically begging her to come back. I'm his only kid, you know? He took that seriously."

"So how would you describe your mom and dad's relationship right now?" Liz asked. "Is it—productive? Would you say your dad is still interested in, ah, holding onto your mother?"

"Nah, I think my dad's kind of moved on by this point," I said. I saw no reason to mention Diane, the skanky Dallas BBQ waitress who'd been hanging around his place the last few times I'd visited.

The last weekend I was in the city, the same trip I bought the D batteries to fill my old sock, Dad and Diane had spent most of Saturday inside the bedroom, with the door closed and the hip-hop music blasting so loudly I wouldn't have been able to hear anything even if I'd wanted to, which I didn't. I'd been hoping to go out and window-shop for some new shoes, but I wasn't about to interrupt whatever nasty business they had going on, and my dad liked when I asked permission before hitting the streets. That was about the only rule he had, which was yet another reason I looked forward to visiting him.

I spent most of Saturday watching Turner Classic Movies, which I could never have done at my mom's place, and not only because she's too cheap to shell out for cable. She's anti-TV, even if the TV I'm watching happens to be prime classic cinema. If nothing else I love weekends at my dad's for his deluxe cable package.

"How'd a good-looking man like you get such a fattie for a kid?" Diane had asked, and I tried not to notice when my dad busted up laughing and told her it was a real good question. But that was always how my dad had acted around the women in his life, including my mom.

In my personal opinion, he let the ladies boss him around a little too much.

"I'd say my mom and dad still get along pretty well," I told Liz. "He's dated a bunch of different women, but no one serious. The same goes for my mom. Even though she's the one who did the dumping, she's stayed single ever since we moved out to Garden City, so I don't know, could be she's still a little hung up on him?"

"I see," said Liz, nodding as if she'd just figured out the answer to some really complicated math problem. She actually reminded me a little of my math teacher Mrs. Fleming that way, and I don't mean that as a compliment. I wondered how many black kids Liz had coming to her "practice"—that's what she called it—and what the rest of them thought of that stupid sailboat painting hanging lopsided over Liz's head. "So you said something earlier about not seeing your Garden City friends much on the weekends. How many weekends a month would you say you spend with your dad?"

"Two," I answered. "I mean, that's what they agreed on when my mom first moved out here, but sometimes it works out to more like . . . The thing is, my dad works a lot, so when he's on a job, it can be hard to take time off. And then my mom is sometimes too busy to drive me into the city—it's not all that close, you know, and she doesn't like me riding the train on my own, which is crazy since in the city I've been riding the subway since I was like six. But anyway, yeah, sometimes it's more like one weekend a month, and sometimes it's three if my mom's working a ton. It really just sort of depends."

Last time I was over there, on Saturday night Dad actually kicked Diane out—which she said was fine because she was working that night anyway, and she made more in one shift than his lazy ass earned in a week—so he could take me to the big Magic Johnson Theater on 125th Street. He told me I could pick out any movie I wanted; I just had to name it.

Another thing about my mom: She *never* takes me to movies. She says they're a big waste of money when you could watch the same crap on TV for free, and a complete waste of time, too. We all knew that time was a pretty precious commodity to my mom, who, ever since she left my dad to "better our lives," spent every second of the day either working a double shift as an orderly at St. Vincent's, or attending a class at nursing school, or studying for a class, or catching up on sleep. There was, she said so herself, very little left afterward.

"How would you say your dad and you spend your weekends together?" Liz asked, still jotting down stupid shit in her notebook. "You guys ever do anything special?"

I shrugged. "Nah, I don't know. We just do—stuff. We hang out with some of my old school friends, and some friends he's made since we left the city"—before Diane there was Tina, and before Tina there was Alexis— "and sometimes we play some b-ball and sometimes we go to the movies. That's what I like best, when he takes me to the movies."

I chose *Battleground: LA* because I'd always been a sucker for post-apocalyptic urban shit, and my dad said okay and bought the tickets. He got us popcorn, which was great even if he felt like he had to add, "I don't think you need the extra butter, boy." When we got inside the theater, we sat down next to each other in the dark, and about five minutes into the previews my dad fell dead asleep. He works really hard, my dad—right now they're putting up a new condo building across the street from Marcus Garvey Park—and he and Diane had been up really late the night before. So I didn't mind at all that he slept for two hours straight and didn't wake up till after the final credits had rolled and the lights had come back on. Earlier he'd said we could grab a couple of burgers on the way home, but sometimes when my dad naps, he has trouble waking up afterward. So instead, after pointing out that my ass sure didn't need another burger on it, anyway, my dad suggested we just head back uptown to have dinner in his apartment.

The only problem was that my dad's refrigerator was completely empty, and there was no food anywhere else in the apartment, either. About thirty seconds after he let us into the apartment, my dad collapsed onto his messy bed and fell right back asleep. I lay awake on the couch for hours afterward, my stomach growling over the background buzz of the city on the other side of the window. But the movie was really great, as good as everyone said for sure. The special effects were just mind-blowing.

When I woke up the Saturday after my first full week back in school, I was surprised to find my mom in the kitchen cooking breakfast in her bathrobe. "Hey, Mom," I said, totally taken aback by the scene before me. "Have I forgotten my own birthday or something?"

She gave me a look and shook her head. "Very funny. No, sweetie. I just thought you might want pancakes this morning, that's all."

I looked around the kitchen, which was crazy tidy, almost sparkling, like in a TV commercial or something. Mom had sure gotten up early. "So you're not working today? Did you get fired? What's up?"

Mom stirred the batter with a wooden spoon. "Ha, ha. No, I took the day off—what's so strange about that? I just feel like I haven't seen enough of you lately."

The thing that was strange about my mom taking the day off was that she hadn't taken a day off in almost two years, not since she'd started studying for her R.N. degree. My mom wanted to be a nurse so bad, she'd work twenty-four-hour shifts as an orderly just to be in the thick of the whole hospital scene she loved so much. So that meant—hmm. I looked at her suspiciously.

She said, "I was thinking we could do something together, just the two of us. Like maybe we could go to the zoo, what do you think?"

Now I *knew* she'd lost it. That, or the school had forced her to spend more time with me as a condition of my "rehabilitation." Seemed like my mom would do anything to keep me out of the expensive Catholic school on the other side of town from Watkins.

"The zoo?" I said. "Mom, I'm 13, not 5. I'm going to high school next year, for crying out loud." And then, for the first time, I looked around the apartment, which seemed tidier than usual, and emptier. "Is Evelyn coming, too?" I asked.

My mom appeared to think this was the craziest

question ever. "No, why would she? Evelyn's visiting family in Jersey this weekend," she said. "I can't remember when she said she'd be back."

Yeah, right. "So that's the deal then? Everyone-spend- time-with-their-family-day, that it?"

"Here, sit down," Mom said, arranging a stack of pancakes on one of our old plates. "I even went out and got new syrup this morning. I hadn't noticed we were out."

That was probably because she hadn't opened a single kitchen cabinet in the almost eighteen months since we'd moved out here. But because I was still treading on thin ice with her after my suspension, I was careful not to say anything that might piss her off. Instead I pulled up a chair to the dinky kitchen table, which was mostly used as a storage surface for all the bills and pizza menus shoved into our little mailbox every day, and dug into the pancakes.

I couldn't remember the last time I'd actually had a meal here, and I'd be lying if I said I wasn't excited to chow down. Because unlike Evelyn, my mom can actually cook, and what's more, she knows what I like to eat. That's the only reason it bothered me that for the last—I don't even know how long—I'd lived off bodega snacks and frozen pizzas, unless of course Evelyn was around to prepare one of her extra-special stews.

"So, Bunny," Mom said, glancing over at me from the stove. "How was your week at school?"

"Fine," I said, then took another big bite. I knew what my mom was going for, but I wasn't taking the bait. I was too busy working my way through that second stack of pancakes.

"I heard that the other boy, that friend of yours . . ."

I didn't even have to shut my mom up because right then her cell phone rang. "Mm-hmm, mm-hmm, yes, all right," she said in her desperate-to-be-a-nurse voice, and even her expression became serious and stern. "Yes, well, of course, I understand."

She hung up the phone and turned off the hob where the last pancake was still sizzling. She walked over to me and pulled up the other rickety chair to the table. "Bunny," she said, "I'm so sorry but—"

I could fill in the rest in my sleep, so I decided to save her the trouble. "Yeah, yeah, I got it. There's been a big emergency and the hospital has a staff shortage and if you don't clock in right this very minute, the whole place will fall apart and burn right to the ground. Is that pretty much the gist?"

Mom sighed and reached out to rub my arms. "Oh, Bunny, I've been looking forward to surprising you all week. But you know I've only been at St. Vincent's for a couple of months, and I already missed all those days when you were home. If they don't think they can lean on me, well, by the time I qualify as a nurse, who knows if they'll want to keep me on there? I mean, in this job market, I really am lucky to have gotten such a great job so close to home. I don't want to take any chances."

"Aight, I got you. It's cool because I already had plans today, anyway."

Mom's face lit up, and she leaned back in her chair as if to inspect me from a new angle. "You did? With who?" She seemed to have forgotten that I was grounded for life.

"Just with some guys, Mom," I said. "You wouldn't know them."

"Oh, well, that's just wonderful, Bunny. I'm so pleased to hear that. Do you need some money?"

I shook my head, but she was already fishing through her wallet. Whoa, this was weird. She took out a ten-dollar bill—a small fortune in the brain of my cheapskate mom—and placed it in front of me on the table. "Here you go, sweetie. Don't spend it all in one place, okay?"

"Thanks, Ma," I grumbled, trying not to let her see me rolling my eyes. "Just send me a text when you're on your way back, will you?"

"You know I always do. It should be before midnight, I promise you that."

Before midnight, I thought. That was just great.

I spent the next four hours editing footage off my camera and wishing I had a real computer to store it all on. Then I could *really* make some cinema. Yeah, right—maybe next lifetime. When I was done, I plopped onto the couch and tried to find something decent to watch on TV. But my mom refuses to spend money on cable, so it was all stupid kids' cartoons and a bunch of old white guys sitting around talking about the state of the world. Sometime around two, when there were no more pancakes in the apartment, I laced up my sneakers and headed outside to see if anything was happening on the mean streets of Garden City. Ha.

I'd been walking up and down Elgin Avenue, filming the shadows my legs made on the cracked sidewalk, when I saw that guy Andres from my class.

"Yo, Butterball!" he called out to me. He was coming out of the Checkers with a big soda cup in his hand. I waited for the light to turn and jogged over toward him.

"Hey, man," he said when I caught up with him. "What's going on?"

"Nothing, man, just roaming the streets," I said. "Heading over to the bodega for a PowerQuench and that's about it."

"I'll come with you," Andres said, and I hoped he didn't see the smile that spread across my face when he clapped me on the shoulder kind of like we was friends. "A bunch of the guys are heading over to the playground to shoot some hoops if you wanted to come with us."

"Yeah, that sounds fun," I said, and it did. But the truth is, I'm a terrible basketball player, like one of the all-time worst. I was bad even before I put on all this extra weight, and now . . . Well, now I couldn't even imagine. "But I hurt my foot when I was suspended," I went on. "I was hanging with my dad in the city and this crazy guy on a motorcycle swerved onto the sidewalk and almost took my foot off."

This had actually happened—but to my dad, and about seven years ago. He still talked about it all the time. Andres, luckily, wasn't paying much attention. He only nodded and said, "Yeah, I'm not playing either. There're gonna be girls there, and I'm putting my energy where it matters."

He laughed and though I didn't really get it, I joined in. Pretty soon we'd walked the four blocks down Elgin that led to the playground of our school, the exact place where Maurice and I had faced off just two weeks—but what felt like a lifetime—ago. It seemed like a kind of weird place to hang out on the weekend, but Garden City isn't that exciting a town, and we had to work with what we got.

When we got there no one was playing basketball. It was just me, Andres, Bobbie, and Darrell, who I didn't know all that well. After we'd sat around for a couple of minutes a group of girls showed up. They all ignored me, of course—Janine went right up to Darrell, who I guess she was dating, and the rest of them huddled on the asphalt a few feet away from us guys, where they proceeded to whisper and stare and giggle every couple of seconds.

I was just standing around, not talking to anyone and wondering if maybe it wasn't such a hot idea for me to have come here, when Nia walked onto the court.

She looked over at me, then just as quickly flicked her eyes away and headed over to join the semicircle of girls. I knew I had to say something to her, but I wasn't sure where to begin, or how. After a few minutes I decided to just ask her directly. What'd I have to lose?

"Yo, Nia, how you doing?" I called over to her.

The group of girls burst into laughter, but not Nia. She just flinched a little before quickly composing her face into a smile. Before, Nia had been the one, the only one, who'd been nice to me, but now she seemed, I don't know, almost frightened.

Andres poked me in the side. "Go on, go talk to her. You can tell she's itching to get down with old Butter-ball!"

I glanced over at Nia again, hoping she hadn't heard. Before Andres could make any other jokes, I went ahead and shuffled over to her. At my approach, her four friends dispersed like birds who'd just had a rock thrown at them.

"You aight?" I said.

She nodded but still wouldn't look at me. "Sure I'm all right. Why wouldn't I be?"

I decided I might as well just come out and say it. "Hey, Nia, that thing you saw?" I said. "It wasn't what you thought. I mean, Maurice and me, we had a private score to settle, that's all. He only got what was coming to him, know what I mean?"

Nia kept her eyes firmly fixed on the asphalt under our feet. "It was awful what you did to him. I mean, what could he possibly have done to deserve *that*? I've known Maurice since kindergarten, and he's always been a nice guy. And now—I mean, you ruined him, Butterball, you know that? He's starting at Strake next week, did you hear? One week back at Watkins and he couldn't handle it. So his parents transferred him out."

I didn't like it, the way Nia was lecturing me, almost like she was Liz or Evelyn or something. It wasn't cool. "Yeah, well, his damn parents can afford it, so lucky for Maurice he finally got his wish. It's always been his dream to go to a fancy school with a bunch of tight-ass kids with their heads buried in books all the time. I mean, really, what could be better for Maurice—a place where he can be surrounded by even *more* white people?"

I laughed at the expression on Nia's face and went on, "I only wished I'd gotten to see him one more time, if you know what I mean, before he took off. See if he'd learned his lesson for good."

Nia had no response to this, but she looked more freaked out by me than ever.

"Hey, Butterball, man, c'mere," Bobbie called out suddenly, and I glanced over toward the basket where he and the guys were still standing in a semicircle. The girls were several few feet away all huddled together. Only me and Nia were on our own, a good distance down the court from the rest of them. She was still looking away from me, so I trotted over to Bobbie and the guys.

"So what were you and Nia talking about so hush-hush like that?" Andres wanted to know.

I shrugged. "Nothing much. Just talking."

"Do you like Nia?" Andres asked me, a smile spreading across his face.

"Yeah. I mean, she's a really nice girl. I like talking to her."

This, for some reason, cracked the boys up. They all exchanged fist bumps, and Bobbie said, "Ah, yeah, *talking* to her. That's what I like to do with the shorties."

But then Andres got serious all of a sudden. "So speaking of Nia," he said, "you know she's got a big party planned two weeks from now, don't you? Her mom's gonna be outta town, so it's gonna be bumping."

"Yeah," I said. "I think I might've heard something about it."

"And do you know who's gonna be at that party?" Andres asked. "You know a guy by the name of Terrence Jackson?"

I shook my head. "Should I?"

"Don't know. He lives around here, but he goes to Central now."

"Yeah, and thank God for that," Bobbie murmured. "I'd kill that mofo dead if I had to see his face every day."

"I'd do the same if someone stole my girl," Darrell said.

"His girl?" I glanced over at Janine, who was against the fence, whispering something into Nia's ear. I saw Nia giggle. "You mean Janine?" I asked.

"Hell, no, I don't mean Janine!" Bobbie said, sounding almost annoyed. "I mean, don't get me wrong, she's a nice enough girl, but Janine's main advantage is that she's around."

"But I thought—"

"Nah, man, I'm talking about Tammy. That girl was *fine*."

"He was psycho over her," Darrell said. "Totally psycho."

"Yeah," Andres said. "The only girl our man ever really liked."

Bobbie exhaled noisily through his mouth. "Yeah, and Terrence started messing around with Tammy behind my back, and no one's ever done that to me before. And now I hear he's got his sights set on Nia—that's how come he's going to her party, you know? To put the moves on her hard."

"So Terrence and Tammy aren't together anymore?" I was having a little trouble following the whole deal.

The boys all exchanged glances. "No, man, aren't you following at all?" Andres said. "A dog like that, he moves fast. He don't stick with any one woman for too long. Terrence is showing up at that party to put the moves on Nia, and there's only one way to stop that from happening." The three of them were looking right at me.

"How's that?" I asked slowly.

"Well, by him getting punished, that's how," Andres said this as if it were the most obvious thing in the world. "By our man Butterball, to be more precise."

"Yeah," Bobbie said, "a nice sock in his teeth might teach that dog a thing or two about whose girls not to mess with."

I remembered that strange sad look that had flickered across Nia's face a few minutes earlier and shook my head. "But Nia's not my girl," I said, and she wouldn't be in a million years. "And I've never even heard of the guy—Terrence, you said his name was? Besides, I'm not even sure if I'm invited yet, you know?"

The boys totally cracked up at this. "Invited?" Andres said. "Are you joking, boy? You mean you're waiting for a card in the mail, like? Oh, man, Butterball, sometimes I gotta wonder about what goes on in that fatass brain of yours."

"That's not what I meant, man," I said, straightening myself up. "It's just that I might be in the city that weekend, that's all. I never know what my schedule with my dad is in advance. He's a busy guy."

"Yeah, well, if you do make the party," Andres said, "just don't forget the batteries, aight? That's all I's saying."

"Yeah, Nia would totally love that shit," Bobbie said. "Show her who's boss."

"Got it," I said. "Show her who's boss. Yeah, I get you."

That Monday, Liz was back at it again with the annoying-ass questions. I swear she could look at me without blinking for what felt like the whole forty-five minutes, and if I was getting used to the ugly sailboat painting, her long-ass stares still wigged me out a little.

"Would you say your mom's schedule makes you unhappy?" Liz asked me for maybe the tenth time since I'd started coming here. For Liz, repetition was really the spice of life.

"Nah, not at all," I said. "I like it, actually, because I get more time to kick back with my friends and shoot my movies and shit like that. Plus it's nice that mom has a little more money than she ever did before. It makes shit more comfortable, you know?"

Not that she usually spent any of her cash on me, I thought, glancing down at my raggedy-ass sneakers. But whatever. Mom truly believed that all her penny-pinching would somehow "open doors" for me in the future, and at least my dad wasn't as tight-fisted with his cash.

Which reminded me: I *had* to ask him for some new shoes. This weekend, I'd bring it up. My dad definitely understood the importance of a man looking his best, or so he was always telling me, and it had been almost a year since I'd asked him to buy me anything. There was no way he could turn me down.

"Tell me, were you ever angry at your mom for packing up your lives and moving out here? Maybe a little in the very beginning?"

I thought about this. "Angry? Nah, I'm not sure I'd use that word. She has her reasons for doing stuff."

"And have the two of you ever talked about what those reasons are? What I mean to say is . . . Well, I'm sensing some anger in you, in the way you talk about your mother and the move out here, and I just wondered if you've ever really had it out with her about your issues."

I shook my head. It really was crazy, the extent to which Liz just didn't get it. "Issues? I don't care what shit you're sensing, but I don't have any issues, lady, I mean Liz. And besides, that's not really my mom's style. What's that thing she always says? Oh, yeah. 'I'm a doer, not a talker.' And that's pretty much true. My mom probably would have driven my dad crazy a lot earlier if she'd been into that touchy-feely shit."

"Do you ever wish your mom was different?" Liz asked. "That she was easier to talk to?"

I scoffed at this. "Why would I? I love my mom, always have and always will. Sure, we have our fights, and yeah, sometimes I'm not as into this town as she is, but so what? Anyway, she's right. It doesn't do anyone any good to talk about stuff, you know?"

"Well, if it doesn't do any good to talk about stuff, then why exactly are you here?" Liz asked.

I mean, damn, would she *never* get it into that brain of hers that I was here because I had to be here? Because I had like the opposite of a choice in the matter?

She must've seen the look on my face because she quickly changed her tune. "A little earlier you said your mom and you fight sometimes. What do you fight about exactly, would you say?"

"I don't know. All kinds of things. Just the regular mom stuff."

"Like what? Can you give me one specific example?"

Liz was really irritating me now. "I told you I don't know! Like, she makes me look stupid sometimes, the way she treats me. And I never can have people over to our place because . . ."

"Because why?" Liz prodded.

"Because she's never around long enough to clean it up and it looks like shit all the time, that's why," I snapped. "You'd think a woman so set on bettering our lives would clean up the kitchen once a month or so, but then you'd be dead wrong. My mom's so busy cleaning up after people at work all the time that she never has time to clean up after herself. At least that's her excuse."

Liz was eyeing me with a new expression, and I realized I'd broken my own rules and let myself get a little heated up. She looked almost proud of herself, and that wasn't gonna fly with me.

"Have you ever talked to her about that?" she asked gently, but I could see through her whole deal. "About how the mess really bothers you?"

"Yo, I'm not saying it bothers me, aight? I'm just saying it's a thing my mom and I fight about sometimes, since you asked for specifics and all. She always says I should start by cleaning up after myself, but that's not really the point, know what I mean? When she lived with my dad, she always kept the place real tidy, but now, well . . . I don't know what's happened to her since then. It's kind of like she's just given up on a bunch of shit."

Liz didn't say anything for a while, almost as if by waiting she'd trick me into talking again. But this time I wasn't having it. I could stare as good as anyone else.

"What else, then? Any other sore subjects?" Liz asked after maybe five minutes of this forced silence. She had her pen poised right over that spiral. But she had another think coming because I was finished.

"Nope, not really. My whole situation is pretty sweet. I mean, in a funny way, my mom and I get along better on account of not seeing each other all that much, you know? We don't get the chance to get up in each other's grill like we used to. I get the best of both worlds, kind of. Relaxing school shit out here, and crazy fun weekends in the city with my dad."

Liz nodded slowly, and to tell the truth she looked a little pissed, though why that could be I had no idea. Then she looked straight at me. "Butterball"—she always drew in a little breath before she could bring herself to say it—"I really believe you wouldn't be coming here if your life were so perfect."

"Yeah?" I met her stare. "That's funny because I'm was pretty sure I was coming here on account of hitting Maurice. I don't know what the hell that has to do with my life one way or another."

"And why exactly did you hit Maurice?" she asked me challengingly. "That's the question we still haven't come close to answering."

"Ah, lady," I said, "I mean, Liz. If you knew that, you'd know everything, wouldn't you? And no offense, but I ain't about to let that happen."

Liz let out a long breath—yep, she'd sure met her match this time—and leaned back in her chair. "All right then," she said. "Let's back up a little. How about you tell me about your first day here? Your first day at Watkins, I mean. Anything stand out for you?"

"What do you mean, my first day at Watkins? That was almost two years ago now. Who remembers that far back?"

"Moving to a new place can be really hard, especially at the beginning."

Man, Liz's pearls of wisdom were really nonstop today! I laughed out loud. "Well, it wasn't for me. I've always been pretty good with meeting people and shit like that."

"So your first day at Watkins was fine?"

"Yeah, of course it was, from what I remember. Isn't that what I just told you? Fine and dandy. Why wouldn't it be?"

I got seated next to Maurice in homeroom because our last names were next to each other in the alphabet, and that's how Mr. Parker did things, like a military drill sergeant. When I walked into the room five minutes late, still clutching that Xeroxed hallway map to my chest— not that it had done much to help me navigate that rat maze of a school—everyone fell silent and just stared. Not even Mr. Parker offered me a smile of welcome. What a way to start seventh grade.

The thing is, it wasn't even the start of seventh grade. School had already been in session for a couple of weeks, but of course my mom had been completely wrapped up in getting out her nursing school applications, and then applying for financial aid when she got accepted into the nursing program at Nassau Community College, and last but not least securing her side job as an orderly at St. Vincent's. She said she'd been focused on finding an apartment zoned to the best possible school district, which was a big joke to anyone who has actually been to J. Watkins.

Nah, I knew how my mom worked, and as usual I'd been nothing but an afterthought in her whole scheme. As if being fat and black in this town didn't put a target on my back already, Mom made sure every single student at Watkins would know I'd just moved here by waiting till early October to transfer me in.

My last year in the city had also been my last year in elementary school, when me and my friends had all been kings of the hill. But at Watkins Junior High, I was less than nothing. Even in the best of circumstances—and mine were the worst—a seventh-grader was the lowest of the low, the very bottom of the heap. And of course I didn't know a single damn person, not just in the school, but in the whole shitty town of Garden City.

When I walked in the room and everyone was just gaping at me, I noticed Nia right away. She was one of only a couple of black kids in the class, sitting right there in the front row with that perfect posture and those liquid black eyes of hers, and when she looked at me that first time, she smiled. That first day at Watkins was brutal, and I think Nia might've been the only one in that whole factory to smile at me like that.

Mr. Parker took his sweet time adjusting his precious seating chart and making everyone move to accommodate the new student, otherwise known as me. He read out my name to the class, and I didn't blink as the usual chorus of giggles filled the room—yet another thing I have to thank my mom for.

After what felt like an eternity, he finally pointed me to the desk in the back row, and I was making my way

through the aisle when someone said, "Watch out, wide load coming through!"

"Yeah, man, what a butterball," someone else said.

I still don't know what genius came up with my name; all I know is that it stuck. The whole class burst out laughing, and I could feel Nia's gentle eyes burning into the back of my skull as I hunched over and continued walking toward the back of the room. Already I hated this place, and I hated my mom for making me come here. And I hated my big ass, even though it wasn't nearly as bad back then as it is now.

"Hey, I'm Maurice," the guy next to me said, and I nodded at him, the only one in the room besides Nia who wasn't cracking up at me. I told him my name, too, but already my fate at Watkins was sealed: I was, and forever more would be, Butterball, the fat black kid who could barely squeeze through the homeroom aisle.

Maurice was a loner just like me, and by the end of that first week we were eating lunch together, always the only two guys at the end of the long table by the recycling bins. Maurice was cool, and he'd seen a lot of movies, too (including *The Dark Knight* at the IMAX, which was awesome). Maurice read constantly, mostly sci-fi fantasy stuff I'd only before known as movies, and studied all the time and actually went around saying that he wanted to be a lawyer one day. So yeah, he was a nerd, but a nice nerd, or that's what I thought in the beginning.

A couple of weeks into seventh grade, Maurice invited me to his place to play video games. His house was really cool—for one thing, because it was a real house, with a yard and a single mailbox and even a flower garden out front, nothing like the crowded walkups I'd lived in my whole life. Maurice's crib was the reason people moved to the suburbs in the first place. My mom's apartment was just as cramped and crowded as any place we'd ever lived in the city. The only difference was that there was never anything cool going down on the other side of the window.

Another thing about Maurice was that his parents were still together. Even in Garden City, that was pretty rare with most of the kids I met. But Maurice's dad always wore crisp button-down shirts and came home from work early, around five, when I was still over playing the X-Box, and asked me questions in a soft voice while his mother cooked dinner from scratch. It was weird, and sometimes Maurice's place felt a little like a movie set, totally removed from reality.

That was almost two years ago now. Like I told Liz,

I can hardly remember any of that shit anymore. It seems like I was born hating Maurice's guts. Everything that came before is just a hazy blur.

My Friday session with Liz let out ten minutes early. "You gonna give my mom a discount for this?" I asked her as I gathered up my backpack.

"What do you mean?" Liz looked at me with a confused expression. I'm telling you, this lady was *slow.*

"I mean like give her 10 percent off or whatever, since you're bailing early?"

"Ah, I see." Liz smiled and said, "I end our sessions when I feel we've reached a natural stopping point. That could be after thirty minutes, or a whole hour. It's really left to my discretion. I think we've made some nice progress today, but you're clearly done. So I see no real need to push it."

Yeah, right. I could tell from all the makeup she'd piled on, and the way her hair was combed and styled instead of just being pulled back into a messy bun, that Liz had plans that evening. I couldn't for the life of me imagine who in a million years would choose to be seen in public with her, even in this shithole of a town, so maybe she was just gonna treat herself to a half-bucket of chicken from the place next door.

Whatever sad old Liz did with herself, I was just happy she'd let me out early. I knew Evelyn was scheduled to pick me up that afternoon, and I didn't feel like making her job any easier than I had to. I just wasn't in the mood to hang around the apartment all night while she folded clothes and stacked up all my personal belongings like she had some right to them.

So I hopped off the couch and, without saying goodbye to Liz, pounded down the staircase and out into the big parking lot. Watkins was just a few blocks away, and school had only let out an hour ago. I figured I'd swing by on my way home, see if anything was going down over at the playground.

Lo and behold, the basketball court was packed with little clusters of people that afternoon, the blacks on one end and all the Hispanic kids on the other. Most of the white kids had gone home already, off to their violin lessons or whatever kind of enriching shit kept them so busy all the time.

I was in a pretty good mood that afternoon, both because Liz had gone easy on me and because I was going to my dad's in the morning. I didn't usually get to visit him so much, but St. Vincent's was more understaffed than usual at the moment, or so my mom kept saying on the phone to him the night before: "Yeah, and you shouldn't be complaining because the more I work, the less money I'll be needing from you." Then she went on in a hushed voice about all the shifts she'd missed while she'd been dragging me from the principal's to the guidance counselor's and finally to Liz's office, as if I hadn't already heard it a hundred times already.

So, yeah, I was pretty pumped to hang with my dad again, and when I walked up to the spot where Andres and some other guys were standing, I told them all about it. "Yep, I go to the city most weekends," I said. "So much more shit to do there."

I could tell Andres and the boys were impressed, and I sort of felt sorry for them. Most kids around here, even the ones who were sure they were badasses, have been stuck in the suburbs all their lives and only get to go into the city on special occasions, like for Christmas shopping and shit like that. I seriously don't know what I'd do if I had to spend every weekend stuck in this crappy little town where there was nothing to do but shoot hoops on an empty basketball court. Boring, boring, boring. It might not seem like much, but at least I *knew* there was life beyond Garden City, Long Island.

"What you guys getting up to in New York town?" Andres asked, clearly jealous.

"Not much," I said. "Shopping for some shoes and shit like that—my dad promised me some new ones."

"It's about time, huh?" Darrell said, and all the boys laughed like this was the most hilarious joke ever, like they'd actually talked about it before. I felt my skin go cold. These shoes were the best ones on earth when I got them, but now—sure, they'd seen better days, but so what?

I looked at Darrell's shoes, off-brand Adidas probably from the same strip mall where Liz had her office, and I said, "Yeah, well, I've just been waiting for the new Foamposites to come out, but they keep selling out faster than I can get to them. I won't wear just anything, you know." Unlike some people, I hope my tone implied.

All of a sudden, I heard my name being called out behind me. I spun around to see none other than Evelyn the Buzzkill standing there, shouting my name—my actual *name*—at the top of her lungs. Let me tell you, I was *pissed*, so pissed I could've taken that PQ bottle in my hand and crushed it against her skull.

"Chill out, woman," I shouted as I trotted over to her. "What do you want, and how'd you find me here, anyway?"

"Dumb luck," Evelyn said without smiling. "Why weren't you waiting outside Ms. Jenner's office like you're supposed to? Your mom will *not* be happy when she finds out I had to go on this little scavenger hunt to track you down."

I decided to play dumb and deny Evelyn the satisfaction she so clearly craved. "Oh, man, I'm real sorry about that," I said, super sweet and innocent-like. "I knew my mom got called into work early today, so I figured I'd just walk straight home on my own. I was just passing by here when I ran into some of my friends."

"I see," Evelyn said skeptically. I could tell she didn't believe me, but she didn't have the balls to fight me on it, which suited my purposes fine. "Well, it's too bad you weren't where you were supposed to be, because now you might miss your train."

"My train?" I repeated. "What do you mean, my train?"

"Yes, as you said, your mom did get called into work today, and it looks like she won't be off till well after midnight. I'd stay and watch you, but I've got a scheduled shift tonight, too, unfortunately."

Evelyn also worked at St. Vincent's, though as an administrator who answered phones and shit like that—not, like my mom, as an orderly with dreams of nursing. That's where she and mom had first met. "Anyway, your father's agreed to watch you tonight, so your mother's asked me to drop you off at the train station. She doesn't want you getting into the city after dark, though, so it's either the four-fifty train or nothing."

I rolled my eyes at my mother's crazy paranoia, but I was too souped to feel any real irritation. My mom *never* let me take the LIRR to the city on my own, though I have no idea why since I'd been riding the subway alone practically since birth. "Aw, I can get to my dad's place blindfolded," I said.

"Well, we'd rather you didn't," Evelyn replied, stern as ever. "So get moving. I already packed your weekend bag and put it in the car, but where's your backpack?"

"Right over there," I said, pointing to where the boys were standing, watching me and Evelyn with way too much interest. "I'll go grab it."

I somehow managed to keep from panting on my jog back over to the boys. "That your mom or something?" Andres asked. "She's fine, ain't she?"

"That lady?" I tried not to puke. "No way she's my mom, and she is *not* fine," I said, reaching down for my stuff. "She's just this annoying woman who helps out while my mom's at work."

"That's funny," he said, "because she sure was busting your balls like she'd given birth to you or something, though she do seem awful young."

"That's 'cause I'm taking the train into the city right now," I said, "and she's bugging out about my missing it."

"But you'll be around next weekend, though, right?" Andres made sure to ask as I backed away from the semicircle.

"Hell, yeah, I'm going," I said without thinking. "Maybe I'll even premiere my shoes there."

"All right then, don't forget your sock and batteries, B-Ball!" Bobbie called. I nodded but didn't turn around, just kept right on walking across the basketball court toward where Evelyn stood waiting for me.

I got to the station with seconds to spare. The train was already there, so Evelyn pressed some cash into my hand and told me to hurry up. I grabbed my bag and jumped out of the car, slamming the door behind me without another word to my pissed-off chauffeur.

I can move pretty fast for a fatass, and I jogged past the station barriers and climbed the two steps up onto the train with maybe ten seconds to spare before it churned into motion. I found an empty row and looked out just in time to see Evelyn walking briskly onto the platform, looking anxiously both ways to make sure I'd boarded. *And what if I hadn't,* I thought smugly as I slid down lower into my window seat. *What was she gonna do then?*

A few minutes into the ride, I noticed that a kid sitting across the aisle kept staring over at me, which I have to admit pissed me off. About the tenth time he looked my way, I bugged out my eyes and raised a fist over my head. His eyes shot right back to the seat back in front of him. A few minutes later, he got up and never came back.

I got off at Penn Station and transferred to the 3 train uptown, just like I'd done a hundred times before. The train was packed at rush hour, but I didn't mind standing and holding onto the handrail. It made me feel alive, invigorated, to be surrounded by so many people who didn't know or care who I was or what my problems were. Everything was more interesting here, even the tired strangers lugging their bags of groceries home. In Garden City, everyone lived all closed off from everyone else, locked inside their cars and all those empty spaced-apart buildings.

When I got off at 148th Street, I wanted to linger but knew my mom would probably be checking in on me, so I hustled straight to my dad's. I arrived at his apartment building only eighty minutes after Evelyn had dropped me off—a record. I rang my dad's bell and waited, but no one buzzed me in. That was strange, but maybe my dad was napping or something. And it was only six ten, and my dad wasn't expecting me till a quarter after, or so Evelyn had said. He was probably on his way back right now.

Over the next half hour, I hit the buzzer maybe a dozen more times before I knew for sure that something was wrong. I couldn't decide what to do, whether to stay or go. Dad was always talking about getting a key made for me, but for some reason he never got around to it. He's a busy guy, I know that as well as anybody.

Just before seven, I gave up and walked over to the bodega, bought myself a PQ and a couple of Snickers bars, and returned to the stoop to wait. I had my camera with me, so I took it out of my pocket and started filming the street scenes taking place five steps down from where I was sitting. There was an old lady pushing an even older shopping cart filled with winter clothing, and a skinny hairless guy yelling into a mouthpiece, and two kids a couple of years younger than me walking about six dogs between them. Put everyone in the frame and it made a great shot. I couldn't wait to show my dad the footage.

I looked at my cell phone: Speaking of my dad, where *was* he? His phone was switched off, so I decided to get up and ring the bell again. He was a pretty heavy sleeper, and it really wasn't like him to forget about me for this long. I wondered if maybe I should call my mom? But no, no, she'd completely freak, and what could she do about it, anyway? I'd rather spend the whole weekend alone on this stoop than under the watchful glare of Evelyn.

I'd just returned from my second trip to the bodega when I ran smack into my dad on the bottom step of his stoop. "Oh, hey, B-Ball man! What're you doing here?"

He was in work clothes—jeans and a dirty, sweat-stained button-down—and carrying a six-pack of beer in a plastic bag. He still had his work goggles around his

neck, and he looked completely exhausted, like the last thing he wanted to do was hang out with his thirteen-year-old son yet again.

"What do you mean? Didn't Mom call you last night?" I'd been in the room at the time so I knew for a fact that she'd called him. "I mean, she, like, got roped into doing double or triple shifts all weekend, so she'd . . ."

My dad put the six-pack down on the top step and struck his forehead. "Shit, son, of course she did. Totally slipped my mind, sorry about that. But you know I'm used to your coming here on Saturdays. A little break in my routine, that's all—it just takes a little adjusting. Lucky we both got here at the same time, though, huh?"

I glanced down at my camera, then shoved it in my pocket. "Yeah," I said. "Real lucky."

"Yo, so listen, I was gonna see Diane later on, but I'm too beat anyway. Let me just call her and cancel, all right?" he said as I followed him up the dark staircase. "You feel like hitting another movie tonight?"

Of course I wanted to hit another movie, but I didn't want to push it, not when I had a much bigger favor to ask of my dad that weekend. "You're sure you're not too tired?"

"Nah, boy, you know I can sleep anywhere."

After a quick shower and change of clothes, my dad and I headed back downstairs. It was totally dark by the time we made it outside. Before getting on the train, we stopped off for some pizza.

We were waiting on the downtown platform, both of us with a slice of pepperoni in each hand, when I decided to ask my dad about the sneakers. "Hey, Dad?" I asked, and he nodded between chews. "Can I ask you a big favor, do you mind? And you can say no; I swear I won't care. It's just, well . . . You see these shoes I'm wearing? Well, they're sort of old and shit, and I don't know . . ."

I'd had a whole speech prepared, but it turned out I didn't need it. "You want some new kicks, my man, is that what you're getting at? Hell, yes, those there are looking nasty. I'll hook you up. We'll hit the shops tomorrow—you want to swing by Atmos first, don't you?"

The whole ride down to 125th Street, I felt like my face was going to split in two from grinning. I couldn't believe I was finally getting me some new shoes! My dad really was the bomb. Man, Andres and Darrell and Bobbie have probably never seen the kind of merchandise they sell at Atmos. Not even the most tripped-out store in the suburbs could touch that shit.

When we were in line for the tickets, my dad must've

seen me tapping my feet and staring down at my raggedy X Series because he said, "Oh, but one thing, boy. I'll only get you the shoes under one condition."

My heart sank right through the shredded-up soles of my shoes. "Yeah, what's that, Dad?"

"Your mom called me in the middle of the night last night, at God knows what time—doesn't that woman know some of us work for a living? I think that's why I forgot you were coming today because I was damn near dead asleep when she called. Anyway, she filled me in on some of the shit that's been going down with you at school. I knew you'd been suspended and shit, but this was the first time she took it upon herself to really acquaint me with all the dirty details."

"Ah," I said, or maybe I just thought it. I'd been wondering when Mom would get around to this. She was too shy to come right out and confront me about the whole Maurice situation, but she knew my dad wouldn't mind kicking my ass hard.

I was scrambling to come up with some excuse for why I'd done what I'd done. But how could I defend myself without getting into the real nitty-gritty? My dad was the last person on the planet I wanted knowing my business. I mean, he'd just lose it completely.

"Here's the thing, man," my dad was saying. "It's cool what you did, you know? A man has his reasons and I respect that. In fact, I was kind of proud of you when she told me—maybe you're not such a worthless fatass after all, you know? But there's just one problem, my brother, and it's a big one."

He paused; I tried to catch my breath. It was taking me a while to process what my dad was saying. What exactly *was* he saying?

"You shouldn't have gotten caught, Butterball, man. I mean, what were you thinking?"

"What?" My head snapped up. "What does *that* mean?"

"Like I said, it's fine to settle scores, but you can't do that shit on the playground with your gym coach and great-aunt Liza watching and shit. I mean, what the hell? That's a good guarantee of getting stopped before you finish the job, you know what I'm saying? You want respect, you write your own rules. That's why you gotta go a little incognito from time to time, know what I mean?"

I thought of Nia's party, just a week away now. With her mom gone for the night, some crazy shit was gonna go down whether I showed up or not. "You mean like at a party?" I asked carefully.

"That's what I'm talking about. That's where you can get the respect without the restraints."

"But what if . . ." I hesitated, then went ahead and explained the whole complicated Bobbie-Terrence situation to my dad. ". . . So yeah, he took this friend of mine's girl, but that was a while ago. And now it sounds like he's got this other chick in his sights—this girl Nia, who's always been real nice to me. So Andres and the other guys, they all say I should punish Terrence for messing with women that don't belong to him."

"Well, shit yeah, you should. No mofo can expect to take another man's lady from him and just get away with that shit. That just ain't how the world works."

I guess I hadn't explained myself right. "But—but I don't even know the guy," I said. "I've never even laid eyes on him. He took this friend of mine's girl, not mine."

"So? A guy stealing someone else's girl—that just ain't cool. You and your friend, you've got a responsibility to show that dude what's what."

"Yeah, but, I mean, shouldn't Bobbie be the one who does it? I mean, he's the one whose girl got stolen, not mine."

"Depends," my dad said. "Depends who wants the

respect more, and who needs it more. You show people you're a force to reckon with, and I promise you shit'll start falling into place for you. Who knows—you might even get yourself a girl, and any brother with titties like yours is gonna need as much help as he can get in that department." My dad thought this was pretty funny.

My cheeks were burning, and I decided to let the subject drop. I looked around me. The line was taking forever, but I guess that's what you get for showing up at nine P.M. on a Friday without tickets. I shifted from one foot to the other and wished I'd never mentioned Bobbie and Terrence to my dad. But at least he hadn't said anything more about not getting me the shoes.

"Here, I'll show you what I mean, boy. You want the world to treat you like a man, you gotta start acting like one. It's really just a question of getting what you want in your sights and just grabbing it. Now just watch and learn."

With that, my dad stepped out of the line and strolled right past the eight or so people who were waiting between us and the ticket counter. At the very front of the line, he edged past a young guy and his girlfriend and said to the woman, "We'll have two tickets for"—then, turning back to me, he shouted—"what was it you wanted to see, B-Ball?"

"Uh—*Source Code*," I squeaked out. All the people between me and the front of the line were grumbling and squawking and turning around to glare at me, but I just kept my eyes on my nasty old shoes.

"Hey, what's up with that?" the guy who'd been at the very front of the line protested, tapping my dad on the shoulder. "That's not cool, man. You just took our place in line."

My dad whipped around and stuck his face right up close to the guy's. He flinched and took a step back.

"Oh, yeah?" Dad said threateningly. "Well, looks like it's my place now, don't it?"

"That'll be twenty-one dollars," the woman in the ticket booth said, and my dad had the cash ready. He took the tickets and—after giving the guy who'd yelled at him a little shove—walked back to where I still stood frozen in place.

"See what I'm talking about, B-ball? Now *that's* how a man gets it done."

Around four p.m. the next day—my dad had never been much of an early riser—we finally rolled out of the apartment to get some grub. I couldn't decide whether I should mention the shoes again. My dad always had good intentions, and when he made a promise he stuck to it. But he could also be pretty forgetful, especially when he was working a lot and tired all the time like he was now.

But as it turned out, my dad hadn't forgotten his promise at all. "You still want to get some new lugs?" he asked me only about a block south of his apartment.

"Yeah!" I said. "Yeah, Dad, that'd be so cool! I need 'em so bad, you really don't even know!"

"Calm down, calm down, boy, we're going."

And so after grabbing some more pizza, we caught the train down to 125th Street, then walked the half-block to Atmos, which was like a giant cathedral filled top to bottom with the coolest sneakers on earth.

We hadn't walked two steps into the store before my eyes landed right on the Air Foamposites display, arranged in a tall pyramid at the center of the room. They even had them in cobalt blue. They were the most beautiful shoes I'd ever seen and then some. I swear if I were rich, I'd own a different color for every day of the week.

"So which ones you like, B-Ball?" my dad asked, following my eyes to the Foamposites. We walked over to the pyramid, and he pointed to the cobalt shoes at the very top. "These?"

"Yeah, but . . . There are a lot of cool shoes in here," I said, quickly scrambling to come up with less pricey alternatives. My dad wasn't a cheap-ass like my mom, but the man wasn't made of money, either. I knew those Foamposites could run upward of three hundred dollars, and even more for the limited-edition colors like the cobalt. There were tons of other cool shoes I'd be happy to wear, like the Air Jordan XIs in red or the all-black Lebron VIIIs. Even the cheapest shoe in the store would look better than my old X Series.

"Yeah, but why settle?" my dad asked. "Remember what I said last night? You get what you want in your sights, and you go for it. You don't let nothing get in your way."

"Uh-huh, but I can always—"

My dad was already shouting at a kid in an Atmos T-shirt. "Hey, c'mere! You work here? We want to try us on some of these shoes."

The kid nodded approvingly, then asked me my size. I had no idea, I told him; I couldn't remember the last time I'd actually tried on new shoes.

So while my dad cruised around the store, pulling shoes off their display shelves and not always returning them, the boy—his name tag said Rodney—sat me down and measured my foot real methodically.

I was a size 10½, which meant I'd grown two whole sizes since I'd bought my X Series. So yeah, I wasn't being a brat or anything. It really was time I got myself some new shoes. The knock-offs my mom was always trying to buy me at Payless didn't count.

The kid picked up the shoes I'd just taken off, their leather worn so thin on the sides it was almost see-through in places, and grinned appreciatively. "These shoes are classics, man," he said, trying not to notice how worn-down they were on the bottom. "I can see why you'd want to hang onto them."

I grinned back. This guy was pretty cool.

"You got any color preferences for the Foamposites?" he asked as he got up.

"Whatever you got," I said, "but I sure wouldn't mind looking at the cobalts."

He came back with the cobalt box open on top of the stack, so of course I couldn't help trying those on first. They fit me perfectly. I took a few steps around the store, and I swear it felt like walking on a mattress. Everything was so squishy and soft and cushioned.

"These the ones?" my dad said, coming over to me as I pulled the shoes off and sifted through the boxes for a more basic color.

"I like them, sure, but there are a lot of other cool ones around," I said. "I saw some nice Air Jordans over there." Those might not be limited-edition, but they couldn't possibly cost more than $150.

"You want to try those, too?" my dad said.

"Yeah, sure," I said, gazing down at the Foamposites on the bench. It sounds crazy to say this about a pair of shoes, but they really were just incredibly beautiful—the way a sunset or the last shot of *Planet of the Apes*, the original I mean, not that remake shit, the way it cuts from the beach to that wide shot of the Statue of Liberty, *that's* beautiful.

"All right, go bring us some of the Air Jordans, too," my dad told Rodney.

As soon as Rodney disappeared behind the velvet curtain, my dad leaned down toward me and said in a low voice, "Remember what I told you last night? About deciding what you want and just going for it?" I nodded, and he went on, "You act like you're in charge, then you're in charge. It's as simple as that. Now I'll see you back at home, sound good?"

As he spoke, my dad stooped down even more, plucked up the shoes I'd just tried on, and just like that he walked calmly out of the store. *What the—?*

I figured it out just about two seconds before Rodney came out of the storeroom, which didn't give me much of a headstart. The next few seconds are a blur in my memory. Rodney looked at my face, then at the empty spot on the bench where the shoes had been, and then out the plate-glass front of the store. My dad was nowhere to be seen, and just as Rodney let out a shout, my panic button went off. I jumped off that bench and—despite the fact that I had only old socks on my feet—I hauled ass right on out of there.

By now an alarm bell was buzzing, and Rodney was hurling himself at me as if in slow motion. But for the first time in my life, I was faster than anyone, and I streaked up 125th Street like my survival depended on it. And maybe it did. Even barefoot like I was, I ran uptown as fast as I'd ever run in my life, but still it was seven whole blocks before I caught up with my dad. I was panting and sweating and as close as I've ever been to a heart attack, but by then I was safe. I'd beat Rodney and all the rest of them, and no one could ever take those shoes off me again. They were mine. I'd earned them fair and square.

That Monday, I sat at Andres's table for the first time. "You have fun in the city?" Darrell asked me, and instead of answering I just stuck out my feet.

"Whoa, those are nice!" Everyone gathered around to admire my Foamposites; a couple of guys even got up to inspect them up close. I had the whole table's attention, and I remembered what my dad had said about getting what I wanted in my sights and then just going for it. He could be wise sometimes, my dad.

Bobbie let out a whistle. "Oh, man, and you got them in the cobalt, too? Aren't those, like, limited edition and shit?"

"Sure are. Like I said, I've just been waiting for them to come out. Not just any shoes are good enough for these feet."

I didn't see any reason to mention the blaring security alarm and all the sweat dripping down my face by the time I finally spotted the backside of my dad strolling casually up Seventh Avenue. I didn't stop running until I was right up there next to him, panting like I was on the verge of a heart attack, every inch of me stinky and sore.

When he saw me, dad clapped me on the back and told me he was proud of me for making it out of there alive: "Very nice work, boy, and I mean no disrespect, but no kid your age should be panting like a dog after running half a block." And then, before he even handed over the shoes, he just broke out laughing. "Oh, man, look at you! If you could only see yourself, boy, god*damn*!"

"Your pops must have some deep pockets," Darrell said.
"He does all right for himself," I said with a shrug.

I didn't feel any need to describe the look on that nice salesguy Rodney's face when, a little too late, he figured out what my dad had done, or how my heart seemed to stop beating for a full minute as I jumped to my feet and made tracks out of that store as fast as these piggy legs could carry me.

Nah, I just shoved another chicken tender into my mouth, stuck my feet out, and said, "Check 'em out, right. Only two stores in the whole country carry these shoes. The rest are all in Japan."

None of the boys could see the thousands of little cuts and blisters covering the bottoms of my feet from running over all those ripped sidewalks and tramping over broken bottles and stray twigs and sharp little pebbles. No one could see the little circles of blood on the insole of my brand-new Foamposites from the fifteen-block walk back to dad's place once he finally handed over my new shoes. Nobody needed to hear about how my dad couldn't stop cracking up the whole way home, saying, "Oh, man, you should've seen the look on your face when I walked on out of there. Man, I'd do it all over again just to get a picture of that shit. I'm telling you, it was classic. And then to see your blubbery ass jiggling all the way up Seventh Avenue like that! Man, maybe I should've borrowed your video camera to make some cinema out of that shit!"

• • •

After a few minutes of ooh-ing and ah-ing, I put my feet under the table and finished up my lunch. "I think next time I'm getting them in that ice-silver color they've got," I said, and Andres and the rest of them looked at me with real respect.

"You're sure gonna tear it up at Nia's place on Saturday," Andres said with a smile. "No shorty can resist shoes like that." I shrugged but didn't say anything.

After lunch I stopped off at the bathroom on my way to math class. I almost never came to this bathroom anymore, but I'd stayed at lunch too long and was in a hurry. Mrs. Fleming was real anal about tardiness, and I didn't want to make my whole academic probation situation any worse than necessary.

The bathroom was in the same hall as my seventh-grade homeroom, a smelly-ass reminder of all those hours I'd spent locked inside the handicapped stall the year before, just counting down the minutes till lunch period was up. That was before I got comfortable around good ol' J. Watkins.

I was at the urinal, just about finished with my business, when these two little kids who were always trying to take over my lunch table walked in. They looked scared when they saw me, and they damn well should've been. I zipped up and clapped my hands together nice and loud as the two of them backed toward the door.

"What's the problem, guys?" I asked, and before they could escape back into the hall, I crossed the room real fast and shoved myself right up into their faces. I don't know why seeing them made me so angry all of a sudden. Maybe it was because they reminded me of what Maurice and I had been like the year before: pathetic losers. Or maybe it was because I had the shoes now—and the status that went with them. Or maybe I didn't need any damn reason.

"You guys following me around or something?" I asked when neither of them answered. Jamal looked like he was about to piss himself right through his pants. Shit was mad funny.

"N-no, of course we're not," the bigger one said. No idea what his name was. He was fat like me, and he always had that kid Jamal next to him like some sort of miniature bodyguard.

"You'd better not be," I said. "Because if I see your ugly faces around here again, I'm gonna get all kinds of mad." I leaned an inch forward until I was right in the fat kid's face. "You'd best be checking yourselves from now on if you know what's good for you."

I slammed the kid against the door and in the same second pushed it open. As I shoved past him to go back into the hall, the kid fell flat on his ass right on the nasty bathroom floor.

Sucker.

My feet still hurt like mofos that afternoon, and the three-block walk from Watkins to Liz's strip mall felt more like a mile. I needed to soak my feet or get some ointment or something when I got home, but I didn't want my mom or, even worse, Evelyn, to ask any questions about the condition of my feet.

Not that either of them ever paid close enough attention to me for that, but still, I wasn't about to take any chances. I knew my mom would kill my dad dead if she'd had any clue what we'd done over the weekend. He hadn't even had to swear me to secrecy. He'd known I wasn't dumb enough to rat him out like that. Besides, my mom was already good and pissed about the new shoes, which I would've stashed under my bed if I hadn't left my backup pair on the floor of Atmos NYC.

I was feeling pretty lowdown when I tromped up that dark stairwell to Liz's office, and I'd be lying if I said she wasn't about the last person on earth I wanted to see right then. Okay, third to last maybe, but definitely in the bottom five.

"How're you doing today?" she asked me as I plopped down onto her nasty brown couch.

I shrugged, then suddenly remembered how she'd booted me out of there early on Friday. "Did you have a nice weekend?" I asked, widening my eyes at her.

Liz straightened up a little. She clearly didn't appreciate having the tables turned on her like that. "I did, thanks."

I raised my left eyebrow at her. I was really enjoying watching the old lady squirm. "Good times Friday night, huh?"

She narrowed her eyes at me. "I suppose so. Why do you ask? You've never taken much interest before. Why now?"

I shrugged. "I wouldn't say I'm interested," I said. "Just making conversation, what's wrong with that? Since when are you the only one allowed to ask questions around here?" I settled back into the couch and kicked my shoes onto the little coffee table between me and Liz. It relieved the pressure on my feet, so I kept them up there and pretended not to notice the stern look the coffee table's owner was shooting me. "Oh, and while I'm at it, Liz, would you mind if I asked you a personal question? You don't have to answer if you don't feel like it. I just kinda feel like asking."

By now she was practically sweating bullets. It was classic. *Not so fun, is it, Liz, when the microscope gets turned on you?* "I . . . suppose so," she said finally.

"All right, then, here goes. You got a boyfriend or a husband or any-thing like that, a special someone who makes you feel all nice inside?"

And here Liz straightened up so tall it was like there was a gun to her head. "I don't really see how that's any of your business," she said sharply.

"Well, you said I could ask," I pointed out, "and that's all I was doing. Anyway, you asked me pretty much the same thing the first time we met."

"Yes, but . . ." Liz was looking at me with a serious expression. "All right, then, I guess that's true. So yes, as a matter of fact, I am seeing someone at the moment. And we did go out on Friday night, as you so cleverly intuited. We went to Connecticut, actually, to a little bed-and-breakfast by the water."

"That sounds hot," I said with maximum sarcasm, but I was actually feeling kind of fond of old Liz for letting me in like that. And, I gotta admit, I was a little proud of her, too. So she had herself a man, did she? Good for her.

"I've never stayed in a hotel before," I said when it became clear that Liz wasn't happy with my first response. "Must be nice." She kept on giving me the silent treatment, so I went on, "I thought I was going to when my grandma died a few years back, since there were so many other relatives coming into Philly for the burial and all. But I ended up just sleeping on the floor of her tiny living room with all my cousins. It was real fun, way better than any hotel. Kinda made me wish I had some brothers and sisters of my own, you know? Seems like everyone else has that, but not ol' Butterball."

"Has what?" Liz asked when I broke off. "Siblings, you mean?"

I shrugged. "Yeah, I guess. Or not exactly that, but . . . you know, just someone to hang with whenever you wanted. Like, someone close to your own age who isn't too busy for you and had to stick it out with you no matter what. My dad always said he'd wanted a shitload of kids, but my mom put the brakes on his plans. She denies it, of course, says it's because we were broke as shit back then and my dad was never around. But I'll bet you anything my mom's the one who's lying. It's just like her to be all selfish about something like that. Even one kid's a little too much for her to deal with most of the time, you know?"

Suddenly I noticed the wide-eyed way Liz was looking at me. She was craned all the way forward, staring at me like I was an exhibit at the science museum or some shit like that. At the same moment, I felt the warm trickle

of tears down the side of my face. *WTF—what was* that *about?* Somehow Liz had conned me into . . . But forget it. No way was I gonna give her the pleasure. After the fight my mom and I had had on Sunday, I never wanted to talk about that woman again. But I wasn't going to tell Liz about that fight.

I sat up real straight in my chair and flicked my eyes over to my new shoes on Liz's coffee table. They were the finest items in that whole shitty room.

"But my dad's like the opposite, you know?" I said in my regular voice again. "He's not selfish at all. He'd do just about anything for me; all I have to do is ask. Like I said, he's the best damn dad in the world. My life would be perfect if I could just go live with him full-time again." And somehow, the more I spoke, the less I could stop the flow of tears down my face. If only my dad could see his fatass wimp of a son now, man, he'd just be thrilled.

"What time is it?" I asked. "Ain't it about time you and I wrapped up?"

Liz slowly lifted her arm and squinted at her old-fashioned wristwatch. Then she shook her head. "No, I'm sorry to say that you haven't even been here twenty minutes," she said, but she didn't sound sorry at all. "Can we—I'd like, if you don't mind, to return to what you were saying earlier about your mom being—what was the word you used?" She pretended to glance at the notebook next to her. "Selfish, I believe you said. Would you care to elaborate a little on that point?"

"No, I don't care to elaborate on that point," I mimicked in the squeakiest old-white-woman voice I could manage. My eyes were dry now, and I knew exactly where I was and what I was doing there.

"All right then." Liz seemed unfazed. "I just—I mean, if you don't mind if I make an observation. Well, it seems to me that your mother isn't all that selfish. I don't know her well personally, of course, but on paper, well, it seems like your mother has sacrificed a great deal for you. Moving out here, to a safer neighborhood and better school district, working so hard for her nursing degree so she can better provide—"

"Let's get some stuff straight, lady," I cut in angrily. I just wasn't in the mood for any of Liz's BS. "The only true thing you said just now is that you don't know my mother all that well. That's what I'd call the biggest understatement ever because you don't know her at *all*. 'On paper'—what does that even mean, anyway? And, by the way, there was nothing wrong with my old school or my old neighborhood in the city. I was happy living there, just like I was happy living with my dad. My mom packed us up and moved us out to this shithole for one reason and one reason alone: because *she* wanted to. That's the only reason she's ever done anything in her whole life, so I don't want to hear your ass lecturing me about all the damn sacrifices she's made on my behalf. She's never done jack shit for me. Do you understand me? So I'm done talking about her, done."

I broke off, a little short of breath, and when I looked over at Liz I realized I'd done it again: I'd played right into that woman's hands. She was smiling and nodding over and over as those stupid-ass tears kept rolling one after the other down my face.

I might be a total whack job for feeling this way, but I always kind of looked forward to seeing my mom after even a short absence. I mean, yeah, we barely ever talked anymore, but she was still my mom, you know? But that Sunday after my visit to the city, she sure didn't waste any time bursting my bubble.

"Your father didn't tell me he was getting you new shoes."

Those were the first words out of her mouth after I slid into her car right outside the train station. She hadn't even said hello to me yet or asked me if I'd had a fun weekend in the city, but at least I was glad she was too tired to notice how I'd hobbled all the way to the car.

"So?" I was staring straight ahead of me. "He's gotta ask your permission for everything he want to do? Didn't you give up those rights when you kicked his ass to the curb?"

My mom exhaled noisily. "That's not what I meant and you know it. I was just making an observation."

"Yeah, well, even if he had asked, I'm sure you wouldn't have remembered. You've been pretty busy lately, I couldn't help noticing."

My mom made another huffing sound and shot me a tired not-this-again look. Well, she was the one who'd started it.

"How much did those shoes cost?" she asked me about half a second later. "I'm just curious."

I looked out the grimy window of her used Honda, which sputtered every time she pumped on the brakes. "No idea," I said. "He told me I could pick out anything I wanted, so I did. He's real cool that way, Dad is. Always has been."

I could hear my mom's quick angry breaths from across the car. "Well, that was very generous of him," she said, "especially since he's three months late on his payments."

"Mom, don't you be talking to me about his pay-ments again. You *know* it's none of my business. Besides, Dad's been picking up a lot of slack from you lately."

"And beyond that," she went on, as if not having heard me, "I have a real problem with your father rewarding you for—for . . ."

Even now she couldn't bring herself to say the words "kicking that poor nerd's ass" out loud. Instead she mumbled quietly to herself, as if I weren't right there next to her, "I told him you were grounded and *this* is what he does? I swear, every single thing I do, that man tries to undermine."

"You have no idea," I murmured, looking down at my Foamposites.

"What was that?" she snapped at me.

"Nothing," I said quickly.

"You *know* I won't have you cursing at me under your breath, young man. You know perfectly well that's never been something I've tolerated."

Man, she was worked up, and we weren't even half-way back from the train station yet. There were big pockets under her eyes from what was probably another long weekend at work. I was feeling pretty tired myself, so I figured I'd better turn down the volume a little. "I wasn't cursing, Ma," I said, then added to be safe, "I promise you. I was just saying that—well, I mean, I really needed to get me some new shoes, so I just asked Dad for a little early birthday present, that's all."

"Four months is pretty early," she said. "And I still don't understand what was wrong with the shoes *I* got you. They're perfectly nice, and they look identical to all the other sneakers you're always going on about."

And though I was doing my best to keep the peace, I just couldn't let this one slide. "They don't look *anything* alike, Ma. How many times do I have to tell you? No one in his right mind would wear those ugly-ass Payless rip-offs in public, not even in this retarded town."

"Don't you dare curse at me, young man!"

"Relax, Ma, I wasn't cursing *at*—"

But it was too late. My mom usually kept a tight lid on her emotions, but when she got pissed, she got *pissed*. No way I could bring her down easily now. "And what does that mean, anyway, you *need* new shoes?" she practically yelled across the car. "What's so important all of a sudden that you've gotta waste money your dad doesn't have on shoes that look just like ones you already have?"

I knew I'd have to ask her sooner or later, and now seemed as good a time as any, since otherwise there was no way she or Evelyn would let me out on Saturday night. Who knows if my mom and I would get a chance to talk between now and then? "Because," I burst out, "a good friend of mine is having a party next weekend, and I really, *really* want to go. And I wanted to look good, you know?"

"You have *got* to be kidding me." My mom shook her head furiously, but I could tell she was a little bit intrigued. "Party" was not a word I'd said much since moving out to Garden City, and neither was "friend."

"What kind of party?" she asked after she'd exhaled through her nostrils a few times. Then, in case I got my hopes up, she added quickly, "And what kind of fool

child on academic probation, just one step away from having his very own police record, thinks I'd let him go to a party?"

"Aw, c'mon, Mom, I really want to go. This real nice girl Nia is turning fourteen, and all the other kids will be there. She's one of the nicest kids at school, and, and . . ."

Was she really going to make me fill in the rest for her? That I hadn't been invited to a party or anything like it in the two long, gloomy years since we'd moved out to this dump?

Mom heard the crack in my voice and seemed to waver, but not for long. "No way, no how," she said, "or not unless I can get this Nia's mother on the phone to tell me about the party herself. Until you learn the difference between right and wrong, you ain't going anywhere until I say so."

Tears sprang to the corners of my eyes. What a perfect end to my weekend in the city. I could *not* believe my mother would actually do this to me. I'd tried to play it positive with her, to let her in a little, but there was just no winning with her. Ever since my week off school, when she'd had to take off all those days from work, she just hadn't stopped making me pay, pay, pay. It wasn't right. I hadn't asked for any of this.

"You know what, I think it's real rich, having you of all people lecturing me about the difference between right and wrong," I said quietly as my mom pulled into the parking lot behind our building.

She slammed hard on the brake, and the hands gripping the steering wheel were shaking. "Me of all people?" she practically yelled. "And what, pray tell, is that supposed to mean?"

I could tell that I'd gotten her good. She whipped around to stare at me, but I was gone. I faced the passenger-side window and just fixed my eyes on the depressing Dumpster where I had to lug the trash every Tuesday night. If I didn't, the garbage would just pile up rotting inside our apartment till the cops came by looking for a corpse.

"You know exactly what I mean," I said quietly as I unbuckled my seatbelt and grabbed my bag. "Try figuring out your own messed-up life first. Then maybe you can start in on mine."

And with that I yanked the car door open and got out. My mom didn't try to stop me. She just sat there behind the steering wheel, gazing blankly at the now-empty passenger seat beside her. She looked like she'd just been socked in the stomach, and that was perfectly all right with me.

Liz, to her credit, let me calm down in my own good time. She didn't even mention my mom again, which I have to say was cool of her. "Do you mind if I ask you about something else, Butterball?" she asked after maybe five minutes had passed.

I lifted my shoulders but didn't say anything.

"All right then," Liz said with that devious calmness of hers. "It's no big deal. I really just wanted to ask you about that little camera you always carry around with you."

"Huh?" Even though I messed around with my video camera on the walk over to Liz's, I was always careful to stash it back in my backpack on my walk up the dark staircase to her office. How'd she seen it?

"I just find it interesting that you've never mentioned it to me," Liz went on without explaining herself. "Do you have a photography class in school?"

I grunted at this. "A *photography* class? At *Watkins?* Lady—Liz—what're you smoking? Have you ever *seen* J. Watkins? It's only a couple of blocks away; you should go have a look sometime. That place is about as likely to have a heated swimming pool as a photo class."

Liz smiled. "That's very funny, Butterball. You have a wonderful sense of humor, do you know that?"

I grunted again but kept my mouth shut. Clearly my moment of weakness a few minutes earlier had given ol' Liz a false sense of intimacy with me.

"Can you tell me about the camera then?" she pressed. "Can I see it?"

I pulled my backpack closer to me and shook my head. What was this woman's problem, anyway? I still didn't understand how she even knew about the camera in the first place, much less why she wanted to see it. "Nah, it's just a camera," I said. "And if you were going to check to see if it was hot, it isn't. I still have the receipt and everything, just in case it breaks and I gotta get it repaired or something."

"Oh, now, Butterball, I wasn't implying anything like that!" Liz exclaimed, and she seemed genuinely shocked by my suggestion. "I just . . . I don't know. I'm just interested in what interests you, that's all."

"Yeah, right."

Soon enough Liz took another approach. "You like going to the movies, don't you?" she asked. "You said that's the thing you enjoy doing most with your dad?"

"What's so wacked about that? Lots of kids like going to the movies."

"Nothing at all," Liz said. "It was just a question. So what's your favorite movie, would you say?"

I shrugged. "I don't know. I like a lot of the comic-book adaptations they've been doing lately, like with special effects but not *only* special effects, also real actors. You know what I mean?"

"I think so. Is there any reason those movies have a special appeal, do you think?"

"Does there always have to be a *reason* for shit?" I asked. I was glad I hadn't told Liz about the other movies I was into—the foreign, artsy shit. It wasn't that I was embarrassed or anything like that, just that Liz was a classic give-an-inch-take-a-mile type, and I didn't want to give her any extra openings. "I mean, why can't I ever just like what I like? I like comic books and graphic novels and shit like that, too, though I'd never really gotten into them until . . ." Until I got to know Maurice, but I saw no reason to go into all that detail. "Anyway, I like reading all that stuff and trying to figure out how it'd work on the screen, know what I'm saying?"

I felt a little more chill now. Movies, that was a safe topic for me, comfortable territory. "I still remember the first movie I ever saw in a theater," I told Liz. "I was like six or seven, I think, and my parents and I—they were still together back then, you know. Anyway, we'd gone down to Philly to visit my grandma, who was already pretty sick, and one night when the whole apartment was filled up with people, my mom just decided to take me out, just for the hell of it. I don't know where my dad was or why he didn't come, but yeah. It was real cool of her—she never does shit like that." *Especially not anymore*, I didn't add.

"The movie was *Batman Begins*, and man, I couldn't even believe how much I loved that shit, like every second of it. I still remember sitting in the dark like that, and thinking how cool it was that no one could see me or tell what I was thinking or even who I was, which I still think is just the coolest feeling in the world. Like I could be anyone, you know? If I stayed in the dark long enough or concentrated hard enough, I could be up there on that screen, too. To be able to make someone else feel that way, I mean, it just blew my mind."

"So that's what you want to do then?" Liz said. "Make movies?"

I grunted for like the tenth time that hour. "Yeah, and I'd also like to go swimming on Jupiter," I said, "but that don't mean either of those things is ever gonna happen."

"Oh, now, Butterball, I wouldn't say that," Liz said. "If you believe in yourself, you know . . ."

"Later on," I went on, cutting Liz off, "when I was at the library at school, I looked Batman up and ended up finding out a bunch of shit about the guy who'd made the latest adaptation. Christopher Nolan, that's his name. I was interested, you know? He was like my opposite in every way—from England, and rich and snooty and all the shit you'd expect, the kind of guy who'd cross to the other side of the street if he saw me coming. But one thing really stuck out for me, and that was that this cat made his first movie when he was seven years old. Isn't that crazy? I mean it was the same age I was then, and that brother had already made a movie? Man. He'd found some camera in his dad's garage and just gone to town with it, and from that point on he always knew he'd make movies one day. Cool, isn't it, knowing something like that?"

"It *is* cool," Liz said, but I barely knew she was there anymore.

"My parents didn't have jack shit in their garage because they didn't even have a garage, but my birthday was coming up. So I worked up the courage to ask them for help getting a little camera of my own. My mom said yes, I could have one, but I'd have to earn it. Typical of my mom, but I wanted it so bad that I agreed to everything she said. She'd started this little system where I'd get a quarter every time I made my bed in the morning or cleaned up the plates after breakfast or whatever. I put all the money in this old lunch box I kept on the bureau in my bedroom, and at the end of every week I'd count up

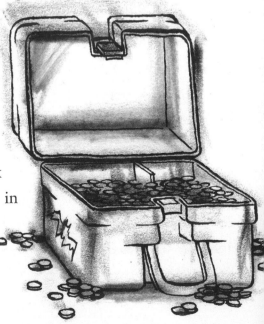

what I'd earned and try to figure out how much longer I'd have to wait before I could score a movie camera of my own."

Liz was no longer trying to interrupt, and that was just fine by me. Man, it seemed like forever ago when I first started stashing quarters in that old Batman lunch-box of mine, which I'd had since kindergarten.

"I'd saved up almost a hundred bucks—it was eighty-nine dollars, to be exact—when one afternoon, my dad came home from work with a brand-new flip cam for me. My mom was so pissed off and went off on him for refusing to teach me the value of hard work, blah, blah, blah, but for once I didn't care. I was just the happiest fool in the whole world that day, you know? I mean, I think it was probably the best day of my life when I held that camera in my hands for the first time. I had my very own movie-making machine *and* a drawer full of quarters that added up to almost a hundred bucks, you know? Just try and stop me. But anyway, I never ended up spending that money, or not for a long time. I just kept on saving it up, and two years later, when my flip cam got jacked on the 2 train, I didn't even care. It was a piece of shit, anyway, and by that point I'd saved enough quarters to hit J&R and get any damn camera I wanted. That's the camera I have now—a Panasonic ultrathin pocket camcorder. I paid for it with my own money, and it still works great. You can, like, edit right on it and everything, don't even need a computer or anything, not that I'd mind having a computer, of course."

When I finally broke off talking, I saw that Liz had a totally stoked look on her face. *Oh, man, I'd done it again, hadn't I?* She'd tricked me twice in one session. "What time is it now?" I asked suddenly. "You said twenty minutes had passed like three hours ago. It's gotta be jailbreak time by now, huh?"

Liz looked at her watch and gave a little jump. "Oh, my, you're right! We've gone about twenty minutes over. I hope this doesn't affect your afternoon."

"Nah, it's cool," I said, but damn was I relieved to be getting to my feet. Liz got up with me. I already knew I was her last appointment of the day.

When I opened the door of Liz's office, Mom was standing right there out in the dark little hall, so close she might've been eavesdropping.

"Hi there, Bunny," she said in a kinda bashful tone— the opposite of the whole ball-busting routine she'd been giving me just the day before. Definitely something suspicious going on.

I winced. Why'd my mom always have to be flip-flopping between such extremes like that?

"You ran over quite a bit in there, didn't you?" she said, but her voice wasn't accusatory like it usually was when I was making her late. "Not that it's a problem. I mean, I got here a little late myself, and I was just a little worried out there in the parking lot. But then I came inside and heard your voices and figured I'd better not disturb you."

"Thanks," I said sarcastically, still trying to figure out how much my mom had heard. "I owe you big time for that because you know there's nothing I'd rather be doing on my Monday afternoon than rapping with old Liz in there. Now c'mon, let's go. No reason to make you any later than you already are."

We were just about at the stairwell when Liz appeared at the door of her office. "Oh, Mrs. King?" she said, patting her hair down like my mom was some kind of VIP guest or something. "Hi there, hi there, it's great to see you," Liz continued when my mom stopped and turned around. She sounded all formal, like a politician or someone on TV. She'd never been that way with me, not even at our first session. "I'm so sorry we ran over like that, but we were having such a productive session that I hated to cut it short. I hope it won't cause any problems for you."

My mom looked from me to Liz, then decided it was all right for her to smile. "No, not at all, not at all, and I'm very happy to hear that," she said. "It certainly sounded productive in there. Not, of course, that I could make out any words. I just meant, you know, from all the talk going on."

My mom was nervous, and I felt uncomfortable watching her. I wished Liz would just let us take off, but I already knew that wasn't Liz's style. "Mrs. King," she said, "I'm really glad we ran into each other because I was going to call you tomorrow to tell you that I think we can scale back the sessions to just once a week from now on. Your son seems to be . . ." she paused to weigh her words ". . . out of the danger zone."

"Well, I'm very happy to hear that," my mom said again. "That's really wonderful."

And I know, for my cheap-ass mom, it was. We're talking about a woman whose whole day gets made when the rotisserie chickens go on sale for $4.99 at Key Food. My mom hated spending her hard-earned money on *anything*, and now Liz was telling her the cost of her screwed-up son's therapy sessions was about to be cut in half. Oh, happy day! That was my mom's version of winning the lottery.

"So I'll see you next Monday then?" Liz said to me.

"Sure, whatever." I shrugged. "All right, Ma, let's go, aight? I'm sure you've gotta a real long to-do list right now and I don't wanna be the one stopping you." I took a step, then another, down the stairs.

"Well, thank you so much, Ms. Jenner," my mom said, and as she followed me down, I caught the heavy-duty look she and Liz exchanged. Man, adults were always doing that kind of shit, like we didn't notice or something, and I was getting sick of it.

When we walked outside, clouds had swept over the sky, obscuring what little light had been peeking down earlier. It was cold and dark, like it was the middle of the night and not just a few hours after school had let out.

My mom didn't say anything on the drive home—no big surprise there—but then I wasn't complaining. I'd take silence over the previous afternoon's blowup anytime. But then, right after she'd pulled into the little parking lot behind our building, she turned off the ignition and looked over at me. "Honey?" she said, quiet and still nervous. "There's something I wanted to talk to you about."

My mom had had more shit she wanted to talk about in the last twenty-four hours than in the last two years, it felt like. But she was being real nice still, probably gloating over all the Liz-money she'd be saving, so I figured I might as well ride it out for a while. I kept my mouth shut.

"I'm . . . I'm proud of you," my mom said after what felt like a two-hour pause. "I wouldn't have believed it myself, but you've really been giving your all to that social worker, haven't you? And I just—well, I just really appreciate that. It's helping us all out a lot."

I didn't want to know what "us" she was referring to, so I said, all sharp and sarcastic, "Pick up a lot of tasty morsels when you press your ear to the door, don't you, Ma?"

I saw her flinch and wished I could've taken back my words. I knew how hard it was for my mom to have conversations like this—almost as hard as it was for me.

"No, of course not!" my mom said. "Ms. Jenner sends progress reports on you to the school, and I get copied in—you know that was the deal from the beginning. And, well, I just have to say, they're getting more and more positive and . . . hopeful. Now if you could only transfer that progress to the classroom, we'd all be in good shape, wouldn't we?"

I gotta say, I was impressed Liz was holding up her end of the deal. If she kept that shit up, I'd have my academic probation lifted in no time flat, and life might even return to normal one day.

"Sweetie," Mom said, and she actually reached across the car to put her hand on my wrist. I shook it off, remembering how she'd gone off on me yesterday.

Mom flinched a little again and pulled her hand back toward her chest. "All I was going to say is that we've— I've decided it's all right for you to go to that girl's party on Saturday. As long as her mother knows you're coming, I won't stand in your way. To tell the truth, I'm pleased, sweetie, I really am, that you seem to be making some friends out here."

I was too busy processing the first part of what my mom had said to react all the way. So I could go to the party without trying any complicated shit on the fire escape? I couldn't believe it. I thought of Nia's face, her gentle smile, and my stomach tossed around like it did when I'd had too many cheese fries.

"Thanks, Mom," I said, and I smiled at her for the first time since I could remember. She smiled back, which was almost as weird.

The week flew by, and that Friday after school I stood at my locker wondering what I was going to do with myself for the next hour. In a way, much as I hated my forty-five-minute sessions with Liz, they at least gave my Monday and Friday afternoons a nice structure. Like I sorta enjoyed having a certain place to be at a certain time: Math lets out, I get my books, I walk to Liz's, I go home. Done and done. I understood better how all those white kids who went to all their clarinet lessons and Cub Scout crap still managed to get better grades than the rest of us poor assholes who don't have all those extra activities. It's because structure just makes life easier somehow. Maybe that was my mom's secret?

I was just slamming my locker shut when I caught sight of Nia walking down the hall from the direction of the gym. I still wasn't sure where I stood with her, but when she saw me, her face broke into a smile and she actually waved at me. My chest clenched up a little as I waved back. Had Nia decided to forgive me, finally, for that whole stupid Maurice showdown?

I felt even more sure of it as she walked right toward me as if there were no other kids in the hall and just said, "Hey, Butterball, how's it going?"

Now, I know this might sound pretty tweaked coming from me, since it's my official nickname and all—and if I'm being perfectly straight, it's probably the nicest one I've ever had—but for some reason I didn't love when Nia called me Butterball. I can't explain why exactly; the word just didn't sound right coming from her lips somehow. I wondered for a second if she even knew what my real name was. By now, even the teachers called me Butterball.

But all I said was "I'm cool. How's it going with you?" It was really crazy, how nice she was being, but maybe that's just how Nia was: too nice to stay mad at anyone for long.

"Okay, I guess," Nia said. "So whatcha doing now?"

"Uh—I'm, um, heading over to the OfficeMax on Franklin," I said, thinking fast. "I'm outta notebooks and shit, and I gotta get some special paper for this stupid life sciences report I'm supposed to do."

I gotta say, I was pretty damn impressed with myself for coming up with such a smooth lie, and without hardly a pause. It was smart for two totally different reasons: one, because Nia was a crack student, almost as much of a nerd as Maurice had been, especially in science. Reason number two was that I happened to know—and not because I'm some sort of crazy-ass stalker, but because the black population of Garden City isn't exactly extensive, and we all live at the same half-a-dozen addresses—that Nia lived in that tall brown-brick building just past the shopping center on Franklin where the biggest office-supply store in Garden City happened to be located. It was the exact opposite direction from my apartment, but I didn't have anywhere particular to be right then.

Nia, innocent girl that she was, clapped her hands together. "Hey, that's lucky!" she said. "That's right near where I live, and I gotta go right home to look after my baby brother. Wanna walk over there together?"

"Yeah, that'd work," I said, my voice all casual and

cool so Nia wouldn't be able to tell how OD excited I was.

One thing I'll say about being fat: It does have a couple of advantages. Most girls ignore you or laugh in your face, but the nice ones, the girls like Nia, they're real friendly to you, even if it's probably just because they don't see you as a threat like other guys. They'll talk to you about shit they'd never say in front of guys they want to get with. Sure, I'd still rather look like Darrell, but it wasn't the worst thing in the world, walking down Franklin Avenue with a girl like Nia at my side, that's all I'm saying.

We exited on the west side of the school, the side that connects to the elementary school that most of my current classmates had gone to since kindergarten. As we walked down the street, neither of us said much, but it wasn't an uncomfortable silence like when I was with my mom, or an angry silence like with Evelyn. We were both just kinda walking along, thinking our thoughts, smiling over at the little kids who were playing on the banged-up graffitied playground.

I realized, as we made our way down the street, that I'd never really been alone with Nia before. And even if it was the middle of the afternoon and on the main drag of Garden City, our walking together like that felt real private in a way, almost intimate.

After a couple of blocks, Nia broke the silence. "Hey, Butterball, can I ask you something?"

"Sure," I said. I was just as happy to talk as not to talk. With Nia at my side, I was just plain happy, end of story.

"You know the party I'm having tomorrow night?"

I nodded: Every black kid in Garden City knew about Nia's party, but this was the first time she'd brought it up directly with me.

"It's actually at my Aunt Cora's house," she said. "She's throwing it for my fourteenth birthday since my mom's place is so small and full up with little kids all the time."

I nodded again, though I hadn't actually known about the aunt. Andres had made the scene sound a little less family-oriented than that.

As if reading my thoughts, Nia went on, "Cora's real young—she just turned twenty-two a few weeks ago. She's like fifteen years younger than my mom, so the two of them were never close as kids, you know? But Cora's always been real sweet to me, taken me under her wing and stuff."

Nia frowned a little, then said, "She's also a little wild, though, and my mom don't like that one bit. I'm not saying she been in trouble with the law or gotten pregnant or nothing like that. But my mom still don't trust her. Thinks Cora's a troublemaker, and says the baby of the family always turns out like that if you don't watch it. Like my youngest brother James—he's the one I'm gonna watch right now—he can barely walk and already he's raising hell wherever he can find it."

"I'd love to meet him sometime," I said, then immediately felt like an idiot. Man, Nia'd be taking out a restraining order against me if I didn't check myself.

But she only flashed another smile. "Yeah, he's a real cutie, little James. I think he'd like you a lot."

"I love babies," I said, though I have no idea why, since I'd spent barely any time with them since my Philly cousins were little. But my mom worked in the neonatal intensive care ward sometimes, and back when she and I used to talk, she was always going on about all the poor little things in there.

"Anyway," Nia said, "Cora's just trying to be nice by throwing a party for her favorite niece, but my mom's all suspicious and shit. She don't like Cora's new boyfriend who she just moved in with, but that's just because he's got lots of money and a crib my mom could only dream of."

"That sounds pretty wacked," I said. For the first time, I started to wonder why exactly Nia was telling me all this.

"So I just don't want anything to get out of hand, right?" Nia said, and suddenly it was all clear to me. Nia was telling me *not* to show up at her aunt's party. I'd gotten permission from my mom and everything, and now the nicest girl in school was pretty much locking the door in my face.

I can't tell you how shitty I felt right then, knowing that was the only reason Nia had walked all those blocks with me. No wonder she'd been quiet earlier. It was because she'd been building up the courage to let me off easy. Man. I stood there, dead still at the intersection of Franklin and Stewart, feeling like the world's biggest asshole. And angry as shit, too.

"Butterball?" Nia said, breaking the spell. "You okay? The light's changed, c'mon."

"Don't you worry about me," I snapped as I followed her out into the street, but Nia didn't seem to notice the bottled-up rage in my voice. I didn't know why I was still walking with her—probably only because I wasn't all that eager to head back home to find Evelyn rifling through my personal possessions under the pretense of "tidying." Tidying my ass. The only thing harder than keeping my cool with the backstabbing Nia was having a civil conversation with Evelyn.

"So yeah," Nia was still talking obliviously on, "I had a little favor to ask you. It sounds kinda weird, but, well, I'd just be real grateful if I mean, if you're coming—and you *are* coming, I hope?—could you, like, help me keep an eye on shit? Make sure nothing gets too out of hand, know what I mean?"

I came to a complete stop again, before we'd finished crossing the street. I was trying to process what exactly Nia was asking of me. She *hoped* I was coming to the party tomorrow night? Had she really just said that? And then, just as she started to look at me funny, I came to my senses and kept walking toward the curb.

"Sorry," I said quickly. "I'm still just getting used to these shoes," and as I spoke, I realized that for the first time all week my feet weren't hurting me one bit. "As for the favor, yeah, sure, I'd be happy to help you out tomorrow night. No problem at all."

"Oh, good," Nia said, smiling over at me. "I knew I could count on you, Butterball. Because if any bad shit goes down, my mom'll have both me and Aunt Cora on lockdown, I'm serious. I'm *so* glad you'll be there. I always knew I could count on you."

We walked on for a few more minutes, and I gotta say, I was feeling like the king of the world himself under that warm spring sun. And then suddenly Nia came to a stop and said, "Well, here we are."

I looked around at the big mall parking lot in front of us, totally confused. "Here we are what?"

"OfficeMax," Nia said, gesturing at the gigantic store like two feet away from us. "Didn't you say you had to get stuff for your science project?"

I saved myself just in time, right as a suspicious little frown crossed Nia's face. "Oh, damn. Guess I was just trying to block that Mrs. Stimpson bitch outta my brain, know what I'm saying?"

I laughed real loud, but Nia was still giving me a kinda funny look. "All right then, check you later," I said, and—because I was kinda embarrassed—I walked right through the double doors of OfficeMax without even turning around to wave goodbye.

I didn't have a penny in my pocket, but then I also didn't have no science project. Besides, if there's one thing my dad had taught me, it was that you didn't need money to get what you wanted out of life.

And what I wanted was . . . well, I wasn't too sure exactly. But Nia's party was just over twenty-four hours away, and I couldn't remember when I'd ever looked forward to anything this much. The weekend ahead was going to kick some serious ass.

I drew the hoodie tight over my ears as I stepped into Liz's office that Monday afternoon. I really didn't feel like hashing it out with the old lady right then, not after all I'd gone through these past couple of days. But the alternative—going home to my mom—was even less appealing.

"Have a seat," Liz said, her voice all concerned and sweet in a way that put me on guard. For a second I wondered if my mom had called her, but nah, that really wasn't Mom's style. "Can I get you anything?"

"Nah, I'm fine," I said, wishing she'd just leave me alone. Wishing everyone would just leave me alone.

"I picked up some bottles of your favorite beverage over the weekend," Liz said, sounding a little bashful. "Just in case you got thirsty. I guess I missed you a little on Friday."

Without raising my eyes, I watched her walk over to the fake wood-paneled mini-fridge she kept over in the corner of the room. She popped open the door and took out a one-liter bottle of PQ. "I knew raspberry was your favorite," she said, coming over to me with the bottle.

"I already got one in my bag," I mumbled, but when she handed me the bottle I didn't refuse it. It felt nice and sweaty in my hands, a whole lot cooler than the drinks that came straight out of the 7-Eleven fridge. I *was* pretty thirsty—I'd had a crazy headache all day—but for a while I just held the bottle between my hands like I hardly knew it was there. Still, I had to admit Liz's little gesture had touched me. I couldn't remember the last time one of my parents had done something spontaneously nice like that.

"Can you tell me what happened?" Liz said as soon as she'd settled into her chair. For a second I regretted taking that drink from her. Nothing in life for free, or whatever my dad was always saying.

"I don't feel like it," I said, the understatement of the year right there.

"I see your eye is swollen," Liz went on. "You look like you've been hit pretty hard."

"Well, no shit," I said. "It's a good thing you've already got a day job because I don't think you'd make a very good cop or private detective or whatever."

Liz still seemed totally unfazed by my attitude. "You also have a lump on your forehead," she observed calmly.

"Damn, so *that's* why I've got such a killer headache," I said, slapping my head right where I'd been kicked. It hurt some, but I didn't show it. "I'd been wondering—thanks for clearing that up for me."

And now, finally, Liz changed up her game. She got all stern and crossed her arms in front of her chest as she said, "Are you going to tell me what happened yourself, or do I have to ask your mom?"

"Ask her whatever you want," I said with a snarl. "That woman don't know shit about what happened, big surprise. She's even stupider than *you* are."

"Well, I guess that means I have to ask you again," Liz said. "It'd be a shame if you refused to answer and had to start coming in here twice a week again. Not a shame from my perspective, of course—I truly enjoy your company. But I know a guy like you, he's got places to be at this hour."

I was squinting at her, trying to figure out what she was doing, whether she was making fun of me or not. Liz wasn't that sharp, but she could be plenty conniving when she wanted to be. "Yeah, right," I grumbled for lack of anything better to say.

"No, I mean it," Liz said. "You're a very entertaining conversationalist, did you know that?"

"Yeah, right." I shrugged, wishing I could get out of there already. My head really was killing me, and I was having trouble keeping a step ahead of old Liz that day. Usually it was no problem, but after the shitty-ass day I'd just had, I wanted nothing more than to pop a few of my mom's backache pills and crawl into bed while it was still light outside.

"So why don't you entertain me," Liz said, "with an account of what exactly happened between last Monday and today to leave you coming in here like this?"

Like what, I almost asked, but on second thought I didn't have the energy. I shook my head and then, after thinking about it for a while, popped open the PQ she'd gotten me. This wasn't going to be fun one way or the other, so I might as well quench my thirst. I took a gigantic glug and then smacked my lips together. Man, that shit tasted good.

"Do you mind if I lie back on this?" I asked, pointing at the stank couch I was sitting on. The thing looked like it'd been on someone's stoop for the last twenty years, getting pissed on by every passing rat, bum, and dog before old Liz took pity and dragged it up to this office. But my head was really pounding now, and even the artificial light in Liz's windowless office was killing my eyes.

This place felt a little like a jail cell, I realized, as Liz said in her best soothing voice, "Of course you can, sweetie. That's just what it's there for. Just make yourself as comfortable as you'd like."

Sweetie? But I wasn't in the mood to pick no fights just then. I just let it go as I kicked up my legs, stretched out, and closed my eyes tight. I was that damn tired.

"I'd been looking forward to this party forever," I said with my eyes still closed, and it was the truth. Especially that last day, after Nia and I had walked to Office-Max together and she'd talked to me like a real friend, like someone she actually trusted. Well, so much for that bullshit.

I'd spent a long time getting ready for the party: showered, patted my hair down, even clipped my fingernails and shit. When your ass is as big as mine is, you have limited options in the wardrobe department, but I did have one old-school pair of baggy jeans that my mom always said looked "slimming." And I'd been saving them all week, along with my South Pole T-shirt that looked as good on me as anything else. I took a damp washcloth to my Foamposites so they'd look brand-new, which I guess they were. When I checked myself out in the mirror, I have to say, I looked kinda good.

My mom insisted on driving me over there, but I told her just to drop me by school instead. "On a Saturday?" she asked a little skeptically. My mom was one of those old-fashioned types who had trouble believing that bad shit went down at school. She was from the time before metal detectors and actually thought school was for learning.

"Yeah," I answered quickly. "The party's just two blocks away from Watkins, so a bunch of my friends and I are meeting on the playground so we can walk over together."

I could tell my mom liked that the party was so close to school, as if the scholarly vibes from Watkins might waft over to us while we were dancing or whatever. "All right then," she said. "If that's what you want."

When my mom pulled the car up to the street side of the playground, a confused expression crossed her face. "There's nobody there," she said.

"Yeah, I'm just a little early," I said. "Don't worry

about it—everyone'll show up soon enough. So go on already, I don't want to make you late for work."

My mom was always looking for permission to go ahead and do what she wanted to do anyway, so she nodded and clicked the doors unlocked. "All right, honey," she said. "Have fun. Just be sure to be home by ten like we agreed on, all right? Evelyn doesn't get off till eleven, but she's coming right by our apartment to make sure you got back okay."

Yeah, sure. More like to patrol my every move and rat me out at her first opportunity. But I kept my thoughts to myself. I was this close to freedom, and I wasn't about to blow it.

As soon as my mom drove off, I started walking over to the other side of the school, for a couple of blocks retracing the route Nia and I had taken the day before. I hadn't lied to my mom about Nia's aunt living real close to school in that nondescript neighborhood with a bunch of one-story houses pushed all close together. But it wasn't true that I was going over there with Andres and the boys. They were all pounding forties over at Darrell's place, and even if they'd invited me I doubt I would've gone. I wanted to be by myself for a while.

To keep from showing up at the party too early, I

walked zigzag for a few minutes, then doubled back to the 7-Eleven on Franklin for some brain food. I picked up a PQ and a king-size Snickers bar and ate them in the parking lot out front before heading back into the neighborhood behind Watkins. I kept on zigzagging back and forth down the streets, always keeping a few blocks away from Cora's street just in case someone spotted me.

The houses around here weren't much to look at—nothing like Maurice's fancy-ass part of town—but still, a house was a house, and any house beat a crammed-full apartment like the one my mom and I shared. No wonder Nia's mom was jealous of her little sister. I would be, too.

Maurice had lived in a house for as long as he could remember, he told me once. They'd moved from his grandparents' place when he was two, pretty soon after his dad had gotten the job at IBM. His neighborhood was one over from Nia's aunt's place, and a whole lot nicer, probably the second-nicest part of Garden City. It was mostly white, too, which could explain why Maurice acted the way he did: He'd always been an outsider. Another problem was that Maurice's parents treated him like the world's biggest genius, so he thought he could say whatever he wanted and get away with it, or more than that—be praised for it. No one had ever called him on his bullshit before, at least not until he met me.

Yeah, Maurice lived in an all-white neighborhood and thought that just because his neighbors didn't double-lock their car doors when they saw him coming, it meant that the whole world had changed. Well, he had no idea what he was talking about, and I was the only one who'd ever bothered teaching him that.

It was dark out now, and I finally decided it'd be safe to head over to the party, so I turned that direction and started walking with more purpose. I was just about half a block away when I heard Andres's voice behind me: "Hey, Butterball, man, wait up!"

I turned to see him, Bobbie, and Darrell weaving up the street toward me. Part of me was relieved that I hadn't gotten to the party too early, and that I wouldn't have to show up alone like the friendless fatass I was. But another part of me felt . . . I can't describe it exactly. Something other than relieved.

"Hey, guys, what's up what's up," I said, fist-bumping all three guys when they caught up to me. Even before any of them had spoken much—and even if I hadn't overheard them discussing their plans at lunch the day before—I would've known they'd been drinking. It was something about how they were laughing too loudly, and for too long, at all sorts of shit that wasn't even a little funny. And something about how Andres kept clapping me on the back, like bumping into me outside of Nia's aunt's house was just about the greatest thing that had ever happened to him.

He even complimented me—"Man, you're sure looking sharp, ain't you?"—and plucked my South Pole shirt between his fingers. "That's a real fly shirt there. Goes great with your shoes."

"Thanks," I said, feeling pretty good as we made our way into the little house.

I've gotta say, given what Nia had told me the day before, the scene wasn't entirely what I'd expected. She'd made it sound like Cora was all edgy and shit, but everyone there was all talking real quiet. And it felt more like a school assembly than a bumping Saturday-night party. There was a big ice-bucket filled with Poland Spring water bottles and Sprites, and the music playing was soft easy-listening shit, like maybe Dionne Warwick or Patti LaBelle. Music my mom listened to back when she had time to listen to music.

After a few minutes, Nia rushed up to say hi. "What's up, guys!" she exclaimed, greeting us all together. Looking at her, you'd never have guessed that the two of us had walked a mile down Franklin Avenue together just the day before. But I didn't mind. I kinda liked having a little secret with her.

"Here, come out back," Nia said, tugging—I couldn't help notice—Darrell by the arm. "My aunt is so cool. She set up a limbo pole for us!"

The boys and I all looked at one another. A limbo pole? What, was Nia turning seven and not fourteen? But still, I gotta say, I thought her innocence was . . . cool. It was one of the qualities that made her so sweet and open with everyone.

"Oh, *man*," Andres grumbled under his breath behind me. "This is one whacked-out party." Bobbie and Darrell grunted their agreement as we followed Nia out back. The yard was barely bigger than my mom's kitchen, but you could tell Cora and her boyfriend took good care of it. There was fresh grass and a couple of big potted plants. From inside the music was playing loud, but not loud enough to piss off the neighbors. It was just the right volume.

"Hey, you want a beer or something?" Darrell asked me under his breath. "I got a whole bunch of them in my bag here."

I shot a glance over at Nia and shook my head. Even if she hadn't been standing right there, my answer would've been the same: "Nah, I'm cool," I said. I'd had sips of my dad's beers all the time. I'd even been drunk before. But in front of Nia, I didn't want to make an ass of myself for no reason.

"You're missing out," Darrell said, reaching into his bag and pulling out three cans of Pabst, which he passed to the other guys. Nia saw him, but didn't seem to care. Darrell was just the kind of guy who could get away with anything in which members of the opposite sex were concerned.

"I'll be back in a while," Nia said after standing out there with us a little longer. "You guys behave now, you promise?"

The boys just laughed, but I nodded and repeated "promise" in a real serious voice.

"The song is tight, don't you think?" Bobbie said as Nia made her way back inside.

He was talking to me, so I said, "Yeah. Real tight." I don't think I'd ever heard the song before, but I definitely liked it.

"Oh, hey, you see who that is standing over there?" Andres asked suddenly. He, too, was looking right at me.

"Guy with the shit-eating grin on his face—you know who that is?"

I both knew and didn't want to know, so I just shrugged as I flicked my eyes over to the guy leaning against the only tree in the backyard.

"Terrence Johnson in the flesh," Darrell said unnecessarily. "What a piece of shit that guy is, damn."

I didn't know what to say, so I just kept on standing there, tapping my foot like I was getting real into the song I'd never heard before. But Andres wasn't going to let me off that easy. He took a big long chug of his beer and made an "aah!" sound, like he'd just finished a race. And then he clapped me right on the back. "I'm still thinking that mofo needs to be taught a real good lesson right about now, wouldn't you say, Butterball? And we're lucky—we mighty, mighty lucky—that we've got just the guy to do it. Don't you think?"

The guy Terrence was laughing real loud and, yeah, he looked like a douchebag, but I'd be lying if I said I felt anything for him in that moment. He was just another tall good-looking guy, and I didn't have no beef with him. I remembered the promise I'd made to Nia the day before and finally met Andres's gaze. It took everything I had in me to say, "Nah, I don't really see the point of it."

Andres hooted at this. He was still staring at me so hard, like in one of those espionage movies in which the CIA interrogators are trying to break the double agent. It was like torture. After too long a pause, Andres echoed, "The point? The *point*, boy? What's that even mean?"

Now all three of them—Andres and Bobbie and Darrell—were all looking right at me. Their eyes were glassy from all the drinks they'd had, and I was starting to feel a little confused. "I—I'm not sure," I said finally. "What I meant was . . . well, I guess I don't really know."

"Well, then how 'bout I spell it out for you, huh?" Darrell said, coming so close I could smell his boozy breath on my face. Andres still had his hand on my back, and I had a claustrophobic sensation, like the walls were closing in on me. "The point," Darrell went on, "is that he stole Tammy from our boy Bobbie, and if you don't watch out, he's gonna steal Nia, too."

I shot my eyes around the backyard to make sure Nia wasn't within hearing range. "What do you mean?" I whisper-hissed. "There's nothing between me and Nia and you know it!"

"Don't you worry, B-ball, man," Andres said, his hand now making smooth stroking motions down my back. "We know your game, and we're all totally cool with it.

Nia's a good pick. You got some fly taste, and not just in shoes. So let's get this party started, what do you say? Show Nia and the rest of us who's boss, what do you say?"

I tried to squirm away, but Andres's grip on my back was firm. It was clear none of them were messing around. "Well," I said finally, "it's too bad, but I didn't bring my batteries tonight. I forgot."

At this, all three boys grinned at me. "You're in luck," Andres said, grinning widest of all, "because *I* didn't. Our asses came prepared." And just like that he reached into the pocket of his hoodie, pulled out a sock, and stuck it right in my hand.

"I got more if you want," Darrell said, pointing at the backpack where he kept the beers.

"Nah," I said. "Thanks, but I think this'll be fine."

As my fingers closed around the sock, I felt the cool weight of the batteries through the cotton, much heavier than what I'd used with Maurice. Andres must've loaded two packs of batteries in there, damn. This thing could do some serious damage.

"C'mon, man," Andres urged, "it was so cool when you jumped that little piece of shit on the playground. We hadn't known what a badass you was before."

As I gripped the sock in my hand, something surged

inside me, and I remembered what my dad had told me at the movie theater that night, about wanting respect. About *needing* it. And I looked over at that guy Terrence and I don't know what happened, but somehow, for a split second there, all I saw was Maurice's face. Maurice the loser, who would never have been invited to this party in a hundred years and who wouldn't have gone even if he had been.

Still, though, I wasn't planning on doing nothing. I hadn't forgotten the promise I'd made Nia the day before. I took that shit seriously, wanted her to know she could count on me.

"Go on, now," Andres was saying, giving my back a shove. "This party's boring as shit. We need ol' Butterball to liven shit up, right, boys?"

Out of the corner of my eye I could see Darrell and Bobbie high-fiving each other, and then another real strange sensation swept over me. It was like my brain was no longer there in Aunt Cora's backyard, but like I was floating ten feet up in the air, looking down at Garden City and all the stupid shit the kids there thought was so important. And Maurice, who thought he knew everything about me but actually knew jack shit. Who'd deserved even worse than he'd gotten.

By the time I strode over to where Terrence stood laughing with his friends, my brain was completely blank. I wasn't thinking nothing at all, not one thing, as I wind-milled my arm back and took a swing right at his face.

And then all time seemed to stop. While my arm was still suspended midair, Terrence gave me a look I'll never be able to erase from my memory no matter how hard I try: It was like even with a sock full of batteries in my hand, I didn't scare him even a little bit. I was the same big fat joke I'd always been.

Then, in the same split second, all slow and casual-like, Terrence ducked, and instead of hitting his face my hand flailed wildly in the air. I lost my balance and went teetering forward into the tree.

That was the last thing I remember clearly. Next thing I knew, I was on the ground, people were laughing, and there were sneakers smashing into my face. Oh, man, the pain, I can't even describe the pain I was feeling, but it was only in my body.

My brain was still far, far away, floating high above everyone's petty little lives, including mine. At some point I heard Nia's voice shouting, "Stop it! Get off him!" then a chorus of other voices saying, "But he started it!" and then, above the rest, a strong male voice—and even in my

messed-up state I knew it had to be Terrence—say, "All right, boys, give it a rest. This blubberbutt ain't worth soiling your shoes on no more."

And then some older dude had me by the collar of my South Pole shirt, and just like that I was out on the street again, alone as I'd ever been in my life. I'd probably been at the party a grand total of three minutes before shit went south.

I was back home by nine o'clock, not like anyone ever came back to check on me.

"Do you have any idea why you might've acted the way you did?"

Liz's voice pierced the darkness. I popped my eyes open and realized where I was all of a sudden. Oh, damn. I didn't know what had come over me, or how long I'd been like that. I felt suddenly embarrassed in that room— dark now, since Liz had dimmed the lights at some point over the last hour. Had I actually fallen asleep? On today of all days, I'd strolled into Liz's office and passed out like an old drunk? Man, sometimes I really did have trouble understanding why I acted like I did.

I rubbed my eyes, still thinking of how I'd floated

over everyone like that, and how I wished I could live my whole life like that, suspended a few feet in the air. Is that what Clark Kent felt like when he walked into the phone booth and came out Superman—that his body no longer belonged to him? Or Spider-Man, who was just a nerdy-ass kid like me before he grew all his extra legs? What happened inside those superheroes as their bodies slipped out from under them and became something totally different—or, like me, did they feel nothing at all?

Nah, I'm just fooling myself. More than usual, I mean. Those guys, they helped people. I don't know what I thought I was doing in Cora's backyard, but it sure wasn't that. And when I woke up yesterday morning and saw my face in the mirror—my eye a shitload more wacked-out-looking than it'd been the night before, so puffed-up I could hardly open it at all—I knew I'd gotten exactly what I deserved.

"You didn't deserve it," Liz said, her voice coming at me from miles away. "Nobody ever deserves to get beat up like that."

Had I really said that shit out loud? I pulled my hand away from my face and shrank into the sofa. I guess it was no big surprise that Liz didn't know what she was talking about. I *had* deserved every kick that had landed on my ass. But Terrence—nah. Terrence was just some guy who'd never done me no harm in his life before I walked up to him with that sock. Like I said, I don't know what I was thinking.

Maurice, well, that was a different deal. Try as I might, I still couldn't feel all that bad for getting even with Maurice like I did. I thought of the first—the only—time I'd had him over to our apartment, and for the millionth time I wondered if I could somehow take back that invitation, lock the deadbolt on him, keep him from seeing whatever he thought he saw. And saying all that shit he'd said. Liz would never understand, so there was no point in my telling her. It was like she could sense how hard just showing up had been for me, how tired I still was, so after all her hooting and hollering, she seemed to make a conscious decision, just this once, to let me off easy. To just let me sit in place and wake up in my own good time while that terrible memory looped over and over in my head.

I'd never had Maurice to my place before because it was so much scummier than his fancy suburban crib, but I'd stayed up late the night before fixing shit up so it'd look as nice as it could look. I'd stacked all of

Mom's nursing textbooks and notebooks and put them on the bureau in her bedroom. Evelyn had even gotten out our old Dirt Devil and cleaned up the floor a little, and when I left for school that morning I'd thought the place didn't look as busted as it usually did. It had looked almost kinda nice.

Anyway I did all that, really knocked myself out, and I'd even gone over to Key Food to fill the kitchen with the kind of healthy shit Maurice's mom always had on hand, orange juice and graham crackers and even those little miniature carrots she kept chilled in the fridge. So yeah, *that's* what I'd been afraid of: that Maurice would see how ghetto we were, how close to coming apart at the seams. It had never occurred to me that he'd see something else in this raggedy-ass apartment, much less run off his mouth about it like he did.

As soon as we'd gone in my bedroom, he'd said, "Now I understand why you've never brought me here before, but I just want you to know I'm cool with it. I'm not like all those other kids at school. My parents are educated, and they've taught me to be accepting of all different types of people."

"What the hell are you talking about?" I asked. Because, like a dumbass, I honestly didn't know.

Maurice had looked me right in the face and said, "I know your mom's gay, Butterball. You could've just told me because I wouldn't have cared." And because he obviously wasn't still looking at my face at the time, he went on, "I think it's really cool, actually. I never would've guessed, but now it kind of makes sense."

I came very close to killing him dead right then, and I might've if not for my mom and Evelyn just on the other side of the wall. I didn't want them to overhear nothing, which was just one of the reasons I wanted Maurice out of the apartment. Just one of the reasons.

What Maurice was saying to me—he was telling lies. Crazy, evil lies. I didn't know what he was talking about. I didn't want to know what he was talking about. I tried to imagine my dad's face if he'd happened to walk in the room at this exact moment . . . if he'd happened to walk in during all sorts of moments that had gone down since we'd moved out here. My dad wouldn't take this shit. Not from my mother, and definitely not from stupid-ass Maurice.

"You know who Miss Stipler is? The wellness counselor?" Maurice asked me a few seconds later. He still wasn't keyed into my state of mind, like not even a little bit. Yeah, I knew who Miss Stipler was—a tiny, muscular woman who dressed like she was in the Army and, even at under five feet tall, looked capable of crushing Mike Tyson in the ring.

"She's a lesbian, too, you know, and she's not embarrassed about it at all," Maurice went on cluelessly. "She has a girlfriend, or partner I guess is the word she used. You should talk to her sometime if you want. She's a nice lady, for real. She taught my health class last year and I liked her a lot. She cared about us kids in a way that not too many teachers at Watkins do, you know?"

By this point I was having trouble breathing. I glared across the room at Maurice, seeing if I could kill him with my eyes like some minor superhero. It didn't work. "Stop talking now, Maurice," I grumbled, low and threatening so he'd know I meant it. I hated him, hated what he was saying, and hated how he wasn't paying attention to me at all, like he'd gone off in his own world and forgotten all about me.

I mean, shit. There was a limit to what I could take, with Maurice and everyone else. I was done with him, done listening to that squeaky know-it-all voice and reading his stupid-ass graphic novels that his rich parents bought him whenever he asked. He could go on and become a lawyer and make a million dollars for all I cared, but I wanted no more part in it.

I got off my bed and walked the three steps toward where Maurice was sitting at my little desk. "Get out of my house," I said, getting all up in his face so he'd get the message fast. You could fit about four Maurices inside my tightest pair of jeans, but somehow in that moment, for just a split second, I was the one afraid of him.

Maurice had all the power now, but what would he do with it? He was a nobody, yeah, but one wrong word from even the biggest nobody in school would be enough—more than enough—to undo everything I'd built out here. And you just could never predict what was going to come out of that smirking, know-it-all mouth next. I thought of my dad again, of what he'd say or do if he found out. Would he blame me? Like getting stuck out here in the middle of nowhere was my choice, or like I wasn't man enough to keep my mom on the straight and narrow. I could just see the look of disgust and disappointment on his face, and I knew it could never, ever happen.

"Hey, relax," Maurice said. "Like I said, I think it's really cool—it's like something you'd see on a TV show, you know? And your mom's girlfriend is *so* pretty, too!"

"She's *not* her girlfriend," I said, my voice barely above a whisper, but all the fury impossible to miss, so that even

Maurice might finally pick up what I was putting down. "And I want you out of this apartment right this second or I swear to God I'll throw you out head first."

Maurice looked at me, and for the first time his eyes got all wide and scared. "Hey, listen, it's no big deal, all right? You don't have to get all pissed at me. I was just saying that if you had any questions or anything, Miss Stipler might—"

"I'm not going to say shit to Miss Stipler," I growled, "and what's more neither is your ass. So get the hell out of here, and I mean now." I grabbed him by the collar and yanked him to his feet.

"All right, all right, man, chill, let go of me!"

When I finally released my grip on his collar, I saw I'd been holding on tight, pulling the shirt so close to his neck that it left a little mark when I let go. We were at the door of the apartment now, and thank God my mom and Evelyn were both in the kitchen, talking and laughing together. My mom never sounded that happy when it was just me around.

I opened the front door of the apartment and shoved Maurice as hard as I could into the hall, then shut the door fast behind him. Then I walked right back into my room and shut that door, too. Didn't want to put no damper on all the fun and games my mom and Evelyn were having.

About two minutes later, I heard a knock and then my mom's voice. "Boys?" she said. "Dinner's ready."

When I shuffled out into the main room, I could tell she was surprised to see me alone, but, being my mom, she held her tongue. Evelyn, as usual, was less discreet. "Where's your friend?" she asked.

"He had to go home," I muttered, thinking, *That asshole is* not *my friend.*

I saw my mom and Evelyn exchange a look. I was getting pretty sick of adults and all their looks, but what could I say about it? Nothing, so I just kept on sitting there on the couch where I ate all my meals. Evelyn and Mom let the subject drop, too, and I thought there might have been some benefits to living in a house where no one ever said shit.

I never spoke to Maurice again, or not directly. He

came up to me a few times in the cafeteria, looking droopy and pathetic, but I never turned around, never even nodded at him in the hall ever again. I decided to just let it all slide until that day about two weeks after his visit to my apartment when I felt a little tap on my shoulder in the cafeteria line.

I turned around but didn't see anyone until I looked down toward my feet. There, about a foot below me, was Miss Stipler, the dyke health teacher Maurice loved so much. She looked like she was hopping the next plane to Afghanistan in these crazy green pants with pockets bulging out everywhere. Even for Watkins, her outfit was crazy as shit.

"Hi there," she said, smiling up at me. "How's it going?"

I gave her a psycho look. Why was this woman talking to me? She'd never had me for a class, and Watkins teachers didn't just go up to kids and randomly talk to them like that.

"I couldn't help but notice your meal selection," she said, and I glanced down at the plastic orange tray in my hands. Four slices of pepperoni pizza, my usual on a Monday. What about it? "And I was just wondering if your mother knows what you're having for lunch today?"

My insides froze, and it all clicked into place. So he'd gone and done it, had he? That little fool. "What does my mom have to do with anything?" I asked gruffly.

"I do counseling for students," she went on. "Free of charge, too, so if you ever need anything, I'm always around. I just wanted you to know that. You can bring your mom, too, if you'd like."

"You'd better leave my mom out of it," I said, backing out of the line as if she'd maced me. A dark burst of hatred flared up in my chest and almost knocked me backward. My dad's face floated through my brain, and I tried to push it away, but not fast enough. *Be a man, be a real man for a change.* The words kept running uselessly through my brain. But how? I had no idea.

I was practically gasping for breath as I threw down my tray and ran straight out of that cafeteria. I had to be alone; I had to figure out exactly what to do, and fast. Only one thing was clear to me right then: Maurice had really stepped in it this time, and damned if I'd let him get away with it.

When I got home from Liz's that night, I was completely drained. It wasn't yet six o'clock, but I felt like I'd been on my feet for days. Sometimes napping does that to me—reminds me of just how tired I was to begin with. I felt groggy and slow and just wanted to go straight to bed.

Liz, at least, had stayed easy on me for the rest of the session. I guess she figured that, with my face all swollen and nasty, I had enough problems without having to go into it with her. "Thanks for letting me sit here," I said as I got up to go. "For not, um, waking me, I mean."

"Anytime, Butterball," Liz said, with a broad smile I couldn't begin to understand.

After I'd come into the living room looking all messed-up on Saturday morning, Mom had made it clear that I was never leaving the apartment again, except for school and Liz. For Mom, it was actually quite a speech, maybe three whole sentences from start to finish: She lets me go to a party despite being grounded, and I reward her trust with a black eye and an egg-shaped lump on my forehead and a flat-out refusal to tell her what had happened? No, sir, she wasn't making *that* mistake again.

So that morning, before dropping me off at school, Mom went door-to-door through the apartment building and asked our neighbors—people she'd never once spoken to before—if they wouldn't mind letting her know if they saw me leaving the house unsupervised at any hour. Those were the exact words she used—talking about her son like he was some kinda parolee who needed to be under surveillance 24-7. That was how low things had gotten.

The one neighbor who I saw took a real pleasure in Mom's request was that little kid Malik's grandmother, who spent most of her days on a cheap folding chair on the sidewalk right outside the basement apartment she shared with him and his mom. Mrs. Rutherford was like one of those stoop-sitting old ladies in Harlem, only in Garden City there was no street life worth watching. She'd had it in for me big time since that night I'd roughed Malik up.

That Monday after my session with Liz, my mom took off soon after she'd dropped me back at home, only this time I knew she wasn't going to work. She was going out with Evelyn. They had "private matters to discuss," she'd said, and I wondered if one of those private matters involved putting me in a military academy or some shit they made scary TV shows about. At this point, I wouldn't put nothing past my mom.

Evelyn had left one of her stews warm on the stovetop for me, along with some tortillas she made herself while waiting for my mom to get back from picking me up. I don't know where a black woman from Newark, New Jersey, learns to make her own tortillas, but I had to admit they were damn good.

Even though I'd never been more beat, I knew I couldn't sleep if I tried, so I decided, a few minutes after my mom and Evelyn took off, to call my dad. Shit was getting so wacked out here, damn. If my dad had any idea, he'd definitely rescue me from the situation. And yeah, so maybe things hadn't gone so great at Nia's party on Saturday, but at least I'd gone for it, just like my dad had told me to do. I might've been outmatched, but I hadn't been afraid. Not at first, anyway.

"Hey, Dad, what's up?" I said when he picked up on like the sixth ring.

"Oh, hey, B-Ball, man," Dad said. He was outside somewhere. I could hear the city sounds I loved so much—honking mostly, and distant shouts—behind him. "Damn, I thought it was Shari calling and almost didn't pick up. No offense intended, but I'm not much in the mood for your mom's bullshit right now."

"She's not here right now," I said. I hadn't spoken to my dad since the Sunday after our trip to Atmos NYC, when he'd ridden the express train all the way down to Penn Station with me. Crazy that was only eight days ago.

"So I just wanted to know, Dad, if maybe I could come see you this week sometime? Like maybe tomorrow?" The thought of going back to Watkins so soon . . . I just couldn't deal with another day like the one I'd just had.

"Tomorrow?" my dad repeated. "Am I smoking crack, or is tomorrow a Tuesday?"

"It is," I said. "But I just really, really want to come

out and see you if that's okay. I won't be any trouble, I swear. You'll hardly know I was there."

"Yeah, well, sorry, B-ball man, but some of us gotta work for a living, know what I'm saying? Only thing you'd be doing here tomorrow is staring at the walls of my apartment all day."

"I wouldn't care," I said, and I was being serious. Staring at the walls in the city was a million times better than staring at them here. It didn't even compare. "I promise I wouldn't care at all."

"Well, you know what, B-Ball, *I* would," my dad said. "Now, it's none of my business to inquire into why you done call me up on a Monday night blubbering like a little baby, but we both know Shari would have my balls in a sling if she thought I had any part in your missing school. So you do what you gotta do, boy, but not on my watch. Oh, hey there, Diane," he shouted suddenly, and the background noises got a lot louder as he took the phone away from his ear.

A few seconds later my dad hung up the phone without waiting for me to reply, and that was just fine with me because my voice wasn't working right anyway. Besides, I had shit to do before Mom and Evelyn got back. I'd hidden the jeans I'd worn on Saturday night in the darkest corner under my bed, but I knew Evelyn would fish them out if I left them there too long.

I went into my bedroom and hunched down to pull them out. They still stank of urine, as if I'd just pissed myself again. As if wetting my pants in front of the whole eighth grade wasn't enough for one lifetime.

I had to wash that shit, destroy the evidence, before Mom and Evelyn got back. I had enough quarters to do a year's worth of laundry in the basement, but for the life of me I couldn't find that damn bottle of Gain my mom usually kept right on top of the fridge. Still, I couldn't risk anyone finding the jeans—I had to take care of them tonight. I considered knocking on a neighbor's door to ask if I could borrow some detergent, but that seemed pretty sketchy. Besides, it wasn't like I was on speaking terms with anyone in the building—especially now, when they'd all had been charged with patrolling my every move.

After a while, I took out the old Batman lunchbox where I was saving cash for a laptop I could edit my movies on and counted out ten dollars. I had no idea how much new detergent cost, but I didn't want to come up short. I could also use another PQ. Even after the liter Liz had gotten me and the one from my backpack I'd drunk on the way home, my throat still felt all scraped dry. Garden City tap water tasted like shit, and of course there was nothing else to drink in the apartment. And yeah, it felt good to sneak out without my mom's permission. If she cared so bad about where I was, then she could've stayed home to watch me herself.

I made it outside without running into anyone in the hall or stairwell, and out on the street Malik's grandmother's chair was empty, too. She was more of a daytime stoop-sitter, Mrs. Rutherford. When it got dark out, she'd usually go inside to sleep or watch TV or whatever it is mean as shit old people did at night.

I walked briskly past my usual bodega, which sold maybe thirty different kinds of beer but not a single bottle of detergent, and headed for the big 7-Eleven behind Watkins. That was probably the closest place that would have detergent, and maybe a little exercise would do me some good, yeah right.

Once I got to the 7-Eleven, I went straight to the refrigerated shelves at the back for my PQ, then wandered around in search of the cleaning products. I'd just turned down the aisle and spotted the big plastic tub of Tide when I ran smack into her.

Nia. I hadn't seen her at school earlier, but to tell the

truth I hadn't exactly been looking for her. I'd pretty much stayed on the down low all day: gotten my lunch from the vending machine outside the teachers' lounge and eaten the three packs of cheese-cracker sandwiches inside the handicapped stall of the seventh-grade bathroom. Just like old times.

I didn't know what Nia was doing in that 7-Eleven on a school night—she lived way on the other side of town—until I saw what she was buying: a big container of bleach and some of that Comet stuff my mom sometimes used to scrub out the bathtub. And then I realized, without even thinking about it, that I'd come within three blocks of her Aunt Cora's house. Nia must still be picking up the mess from Saturday night. I didn't know much of what had gone down after Cora's boyfriend had kicked me to the curb, but I'm pretty sure it was no limbo-dancing.

My already-dry throat felt like it was filled with sand as I said, "Oh, hey there, Nia, um, how's it going?"

And then she looked right at me, and man, I can't even begin to describe the flashing hatred I saw in her eyes. I couldn't remember the last time *I'd* felt like that about someone—well, except for Maurice, but everything about Maurice felt far away now, like a scene in a movie I'd only half-watched while doing homework.

"How do you think it's going?" she snapped after a second.

"I'm sorry, Nia," I mumbled, eyes on my feet. I didn't know what else to say.

"Sorry for what?" she asked. "For ruining my whole party just for the hell of it? For getting me in trouble with my mom *and* my aunt for no reason at all?"

"It wasn't for no reason," I said. "You don't understand, I—"

"I don't *understand*?" she repeated incredulously. "Right, kind of like I didn't understand what made you bash poor Maurice's face in?" Nia was practically screaming, and when I looked up I saw her friend Imani at the end of the aisle, watching us through the display of week-old rotating hotdogs. I don't know why that bothered me, knowing Nia was putting on a show for Imani, too.

"Yeah, Butterball," Nia said, "I guess that's true. I don't understand you for shit. I don't understand why a guy who was so nice and always had the coolest ideas when he sat across from me in art class last year has turned into this crazy-ass psychopath who walks around jumping complete strangers just because he feels like it. And do you know what? I don't want to understand no more. I'm done trying with you."

"B-but," I sputtered out, "that guy Terrence, you have no idea what he's like."

And suddenly Nia was right up in my face, poking her finger into my chest. I'd never noticed how tall she was before. She almost came up to eye-level with me. "Oh, *really*?" she was all-out shouting. "*I* don't know Terrence? That's funny because he's lived in my building since we was two years old! Five floors up from me, my whole damn life. His mom and mine are like sisters, and you're telling *me* I don't know Terrence? Nuh-uh"—she was shaking her head, still poking me hard—"you're the one who don't know Terrence! He said the first time

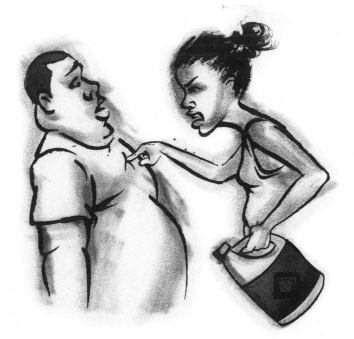

he'd ever seen you was when you tried to pound him with that sock of batteries! I'm sorry his friends kicked you, but shit, you deserved a lot worse if you ask me. I picked up that sock later—you could have killed him, Butterball! And right after I asked you to help me out, too! What were you even *thinking*?"

But then she made a huffing sound and backed away from me suddenly. "Never mind. Don't answer that. Like I said, I'm done trying to understand that shit. I don't care. I'm done, done, *done*."

"I'm sorry, Nia," I said, my voice barely above a whisper.

"Yeah, well, I'm sorry, too," she said. "Sorry for believing you were something other than what you acted like. I'll never make *that* mistake again."

And before I could say another word, Nia spun around and marched up to the register, where the Pakistani man behind the counter was watching the takedown like it was the most entertaining shit he'd ever seen. Nia paid for her stuff and stormed back out into the parking lot with Imani. Neither of them glanced back at me even once.

My mind was racing, and I could hardly breathe. Nothing made any sense at all. Terrence lived in Nia's building?

She'd known him since they were two? That wasn't what Andres had made it sound like, but I realized it didn't much matter one way or the other. Nothing mattered for shit. Like Nia had said, I was done, done, done.

I counted down from ninety after Nia and Imani left before approaching the register. The last thing I wanted to do was look that checkout guy in the face, but I needed to buy the damn detergent. I left the PQ behind, though. For some reason, I just wasn't all that thirsty anymore.

·

I made it all the way to Wednesday afternoon before I ran into Andres and his posse again. "Well, well, well," he said, coming right up to me in the hall by my locker. "If it isn't old Blubberbutt."

The boys cracked up at this; I knew none of them would've forgotten the name Terrence had used before scooping my pee-soaked ass off the ground on Saturday.

"Hey, guys," I mumbled. "What's going on?" I knew this first meeting wasn't going to be all that fun, but I guess it was better just to get it over with. Like I had any choice in the matter.

Darrell and Bobbie were staring hard at me, waiting,

as always, for a prompt from their leader. I slammed my locker shut and headed down the hall as fast as I could. I knew the boys were right behind me, but I tried to pretend like I didn't care. And in some way, I kinda didn't.

"So what happened to you Saturday night?" Andres asked as I came close to the exit by the gym. He slipped between me and the door, Darrell and Bobbie right at his flanks like his own personal bodyguard detail.

"What do you mean, what happened?" I asked, trying to play it off all innocent-like. I knew I'd made a fool of myself at that party, but I felt like I'd already been punished enough for it. More than enough.

"You sure don't put up much of a fight, do you?" Andres asked, and the boys cracked up again. "I mean, unless crying like a girl and pissing all over yourself counts. Oh, man, I'd never seen anything so crazy!"

"Yeah, man, your little show sure turned that party around fast," Darrell said.

The boys kept on laughing, and I felt sick at the reminder of what exactly had gone down after I'd missed Terrence's face and stumbled forward into the tree. It took about half a second for Terrence's friend to land that first punch to my face, and even if he was only using his fist, I can't imagine a sock full of batteries hurting half that much.

Now Bobbie spoke for the first time. "You was supposed to show that dude a lesson," he said, "and instead you ended up being another notch in his belt. You even made him look *good* for stopping shit when he did, when anyone else would've wiped the goddamned ground with your blood, know what I'm saying? And that's what pissed me off the most, I'll be honest. That's what really makes me want to get even with *you* now."

Something in his voice made me look up at him. Bobbie never said much, but he always meant every word, so when he wound his arm back and lunged forward at me, I let out a squeal. Bobbie dropped his arm about an inch from my face, and everyone busted up laughing again, including some kids I'd never seen before who'd gathered to watch.

"Damn," Andres said, "you have gots to chill, man. We was just messing with you, B-ball! My man Bobbie is a lover, not a fighter, know what I'm saying?"

The three of them traded high-fives and fist bumps while I just stood there crumpled against the exit door. In a way I wish Bobbie *had* hit me straight on. A blow to the head couldn't make me feel any worse.

"C'mon, boys, let's get outta here," Andres said. Darrell and Bobbie both stepped back from where they'd been pressing into me, and just like that the three of them started walking back toward the other exit door that led to the playground.

"Man, we should've known that fatass wasn't up to no real opponent," Andres mumbled loudly as they made their way out. "Only kids he can fight weigh like 120 on a good day."

"Yeah," Darrell said, "and Blubberbutt could've just sat his big ass on that kid, and he'd be deader than dead. He didn't need no batteries for that one."

The boys laughed again, and I just stood there, back against the wall, until they'd rounded the corner and were out of sight. I knew they were talking about Maurice, who was as little and scrawny as I was big and fat.

But one thing about Maurice, I realized as I stood there waiting for the hall noises to fade out and all the kids to stop their staring, he was no coward. When I'd gone up to him in the playground that day, he'd barely blinked. He'd never cried, never shouted out, never done nothing, not even as those batteries came right down in his face. He'd just stood there and taken it. He'd been a real man about it in his way, Maurice.

Big surprise, Liz bumped me back up to two sessions a week, but I'd be lying if I said I was upset when my mom broke the news to me. In some jacked way, I was kinda relieved, especially since, by the time that Friday rolled around, I felt like I'd survived a week at war. Watkins had never been this bad, not even when I'd first gotten there and didn't know a damn soul. People treated me like I was the scum of the earth, the lowest of the low. It'd been a whole lot better when they'd just ignored me, or called me fat and moved on with their lives. But now there seemed to be an intensity of focus on me, everywhere I went. Every class, every hallway,

every stairwell: always those horrible whispers, that cackling laughter. Even that kid Jamal had laughed in my face when I'd run into him in the seventh-grade bathroom after one of my lunches in there. *Jamal.* I would've kicked his ass, but I just didn't have the energy. I didn't have the energy for much of anything anymore.

So yeah, when I got to Liz's that Friday afternoon, it almost felt like—I don't know—a homecoming in a way. Even if it was because she was paid to do it, Liz was at least nice to me. Or didn't laugh at me. And at this point I'd take whatever I could get.

My face must've told the tale all right because when I walked in there, she didn't start in on me right away like she usually did. She just gave me a kinda sad smile and moved over to her mini-fridge to get me my PQ. This time I opened it right away. After all my lunches in the handicapped stall, I was hungry pretty much around the clock.

"So, how was the rest of the week in school?" Liz asked me, but gently, as if she already knew what the answer would be.

I lifted my shoulders and bowed my head.

"That bad, huh?"

"Yeah," I said. "As bad as it gets."

"I'm sorry to hear that," she said. "Are you spending this weekend at your dad's, I assume?"

I shook my head. "Nah."

"But this is one of your scheduled weekends, isn't it?" Liz persisted, I have no idea why.

I mean, yeah, I was glad she'd decided not to grill me about the details of what had gone down at Watkins, but I really didn't understand what my dad had to do with anything. "I've got shit to do around here," I told her. "This weekend my mom needs my help doing some stuff around the house, so I said I'd stay. And besides, I told you me and him don't work on a strict calendar like that. I go when it works. When it doesn't, I don't."

"What kind of stuff are you planning to do with your mom?" Liz asked. I looked over at her suspiciously. I wondered for the first time how much she knew. Did she know what my mom and Evelyn had discussed over dinner on Monday night?

I took a deep breath and figured I might as well tell Liz. It was easier than getting into the nitty-gritty of what had gone down at Watkins all week. And so I began.

"My mom has this friend," I said carefully. "Evelyn her name is? Anyway, she helps out when my mom's working, and sometimes she comes by and picks me up here after my sessions with you." I stopped and waited, for what I don't know.

"Yes," Liz said, "I believe I've seen her a few times when I've closed up behind you. I admit I've wondered who she was to you."

Who she was to me. Liz had a funny way of putting shit sometimes. Who was Evelyn to me, anyway? I had no clue. "Yeah, well," I said, "when they came home from dinner on Monday, they told me . . . well, they told me they'd decided that Evelyn would be moving in with us. To save money and shit like that. Plus, my mom thought that I should have someone else around to help monitor my every move."

"I see," Liz said. She hadn't blinked: It was like I'd

just told her my mom had ordered pizza for dinner. No reaction at all.

"And it sure feels like Evelyn's around 24-7 as it is, but she lives all the way out in Hempstead. And the hospital they both work at is a lot closer to our place, and Mom said there was no use in her driving all the way out here when she could just as easily . . ." I broke off, trying to figure out what came next. It was all so jumbled-up in my mind. "Anyway, well, the thing is, our place—the apartment my mom and I live in, right?—well, it's only two bedrooms, if you know what I'm saying."

Liz nodded again, but she still showed no signs of being all that blown away by, or even all that interested in, what I was telling her. Did I really have to spell it out for her even clearer? But then she did the dirty work for me. She looked me straight in the eyes and said, "What you're saying is that Evelyn will be moving into your mother's bedroom."

I felt my face go all hot as those same humiliating tears sprang to the corners of my eyes. "Yes, that's what I was saying," I said in the quietest ever voice. I was having trouble understanding why Liz didn't seem a little more into what I was telling her—I mean, this must feel like a big breakthrough, right? But she just seemed kinda bored by the whole thing. It made no sense.

"My mom's been happy as shit all week," I said. "Humming in the shower and all that. I mean, this has been the worst damn week of my whole life, and she's walking around like she's just been made queen or something." I paused, shuddered. "It's disgusting."

"I see," Liz said for the millionth time, still nodding over and over. "So this angers you, does it? Your mother's happiness?"

"Damn, lady, haven't you been listening to a single word I've said? No, it doesn't *anger* me. It's just that the one time in my whole life I might want my mom to be around a little, she's just completely checked out, and this time she can't blame her school or her job or all her other stupid-ass attempts to improve our shitty lives, know what I mean? I mean, it's bad enough that she . . . But if people found out about her, if . . . whatever the word you used— her *happiness*—got out, it would ruin me at Watkins, don't you understand that? I mean, if it were possible for my life to be any more ruined than it already is, which it isn't. Everything that's already happened to me out here would be a joke in comparison, you have no idea."

I hope Liz didn't see me cringe as I all of a sudden remembered the months before we left Harlem and came out here. I used to hear her in the shower a lot then, too, but it was a whole different sound. Not whistling, but more like crying. She'd gone in there just about every morning, it felt like, while my dad was still sleeping and I was still pretending to sleep, and she'd just bawl and bawl like the whole world was coming to an end right in front of her. After she'd calm down and I'd go out into the kitchen, she'd come in like everything was totally normal. And even though our apartment was a shoebox, I'd act like everything was normal, too, like I didn't know what was going on in the bathroom, just like I'd act like I didn't hear the way she and my dad screamed and carried on till past midnight every night. And even though both of us were pretty good at pretending stuff was okay, I guess we both knew it couldn't go on that way forever.

And it hadn't.

"When is your mom's friend moving in?" Liz asked.

"This weekend," I said. "Kinda interesting, don't you think? I mean, it's almost like they'd made the big decision a whole lot earlier than this past Monday." I shook my head and went on, "And now, as part of my punishment for getting beat up, I'm supposed to spend all of tomorrow and Sunday lugging all of Evelyn's shit over from Hempstead. My mom's acting like she's being all generous to let me out of the apartment at all when we all know it's just that she's too cheap to hire a real mover. But hey, I guess it's something to do."

Liz nodded, but it didn't seem like she had anything to add.

Well, that made two of us then.

"So how was the big move?" Liz asked when I got to her office on Monday afternoon.

"It was fine," I said. And it was, at least compared to some other shit. Anything to stay the hell away from Watkins and, well—the other thing I just couldn't think about. Not now, maybe not ever. I suddenly noticed Liz looking at me funny, so I added quickly, "I mean, it ended up being a lot less work than my mom had made out."

Evelyn's place in West Hempstead had been tiny—a single room with barely any furniture in it. The whole studio was white and simple and clean, like a set from a European movie or something. My mom's furniture, a lot of which she'd dragged up from Philly after my grandma's funeral, was all heavy and dark and way too big for our apartment.

"My thighs are sore as shit, though," I said. "I hadn't got that much exercise since they shut down P.E. at my old school in Harlem. But yeah, the good thing was that we finished up Saturday afternoon, and to thank me for all my help, my mom said I could choose any restaurant I wanted. So I picked Houston's over in the Roosevelt Field mall because I'd always wanted to try that place." And, I didn't add, it was on the other side of town from Watkins, so no chance of our running into any familiar faces.

"Was it good?" Liz said.

I shrugged. "Yeah, it was all right. I got a big burger and some apple-walnut cobbler for dessert, and yeah, I liked it just fine. The funny thing is that Evelyn got a burger, too. A bacon cheeseburger."

"Why's that funny?" Liz wanted to know.

"Oh, just because she's always making these crazy vegetable stews that look like vomit and have no fat or taste or anything. But yeah, she ate up every bite of that burger and half of my mom's fries, too. Tiny lady like that, I didn't know she had it in her."

"It sounds like you really had fun," Liz said.

"I didn't say I had *fun*," I corrected her. "I said it was all right, especially since we finished up early and I got to eat a real meal for a change. But yeah, my mom was all laughing and shit, and I guess Evelyn isn't so bad when she lets herself loosen up a little. Most of the time, she walks around like there's a big baseball bat rammed up her ass."

Liz smiled, then quickly pretended she hadn't. It was good one of us had something to smile about because it sure wasn't me.

"By yesterday everything was pretty much back to normal," I went on. "My mom got called into work before I'd even woken up, and I spent the whole day locked up in that apartment while Evelyn ran around arranging shit and ignoring me unless she needed help moving furniture. I like it better when I can just chill there by my own self, you know what I mean? And Evelyn don't talk much when my mom's not around," I said. "It's weird. She likes watching TV, though, and that's good because my mom's all psycho about that shit and never lets me."

In fact, the first thing I'd noticed when I walked into Evelyn's place in West Hempstead was the big shelf filled with DVDs. She had a ton of them, more than I'd ever seen outside the video store—a bunch of classics, plus plenty of shit I'd never heard of before. I hadn't been able to hide how surprised I'd been. "I never knew you liked movies," I said.

Evelyn just shrugged, her face expressionless as ever. "Well, you never asked, did you?"

I had no response and just turned to check out the sweet TV set Evelyn had hooked up to the wall. It was flatscreen, and like fifty inches across. Damn. I sure hoped that'd be making the move to Garden City with us.

"No way I spend that much on a TV and live without cable," Evelyn had said at Houston's that night, and I loved how pissed my mom was. But she was halfway through her second glass of sparkling wine and not much in the mood to throw down.

"Just as long as we're clear that my son won't be watching trash when I'm not around," my mom mumbled. "He's got enough problems already."

"Don't worry," Evelyn said. "There're enough high-quality shows on the TV these days to keep him off the streets. I'll make sure Burton only gets exposed to the good stuff."

My mouth dropped open. If only I'd had a cocktail of my own right then. No way would Evelyn get away with that. She thinks just because she's sharing my mom's bed, she can all of a sudden call me by the stupid-ass name that *only* my mother was allowed to use, and that was only because I didn't have a choice in the matter?

My own father hated my name, and said so whenever he got a chance. "Don't know what I was thinking, letting Shari name my only son after her dead granddaddy. But let me tell you, your mom was fine back in the day, and she used it to get whatever she wanted out of my ass."

"We're getting cable," I told Liz. "And Internet, too. My mom never saw the need for it before, but Evelyn works from home sometimes so she said that was a—what was the word?—a non-negotiable. Which seems only fair, I guess. I mean, if this woman is going to come in and ruin my life, I might as well go down watching some HBO, know what I mean?"

Liz knitted her brow and looked like she was going to say something, but after a moment she changed her mind. "Yes, I suppose that is a silver lining," she said. "You seem to be adapting well to all these changes, Butterball. I have to say, I'm proud of you."

"You shouldn't be *proud* of me," I said. "That's the very last thing you should be."

"What do you mean?" Liz said, perking up. She was clearly pumped.

But I only shook my head and didn't say anything. *Don't blow it now, Butterball.* Liz was this close to writing me a good report. As long as she didn't find out what had happened in the cafeteria that day, I was fine with her thinking whatever she wanted about me.

But then, I'm not sure why, I couldn't help myself.

"I found out today that I beat up Maurice for no reason at all. I mean—the reason I thought I'd beat him up turned out to be wrong. And I don't know why, but I feel like crap about it."

Liz pursed her lips and looked at me with a little sideways smile. "There's never any right reason to beat someone up, Butterball. Whatever Maurice did, beating him up was not the answer."

"But aren't you listening to me?" I said. "He didn't *do* anything, that's what I'm trying to tell you. Whatever, never mind. I shouldn't have said anything."

"For what it's worth," Liz said, "I'm really glad you did."

"Yeah, whatever," I said. There was no way Liz would begin to understand what had gone down, anyway. Sometimes old Liz just didn't have a clue.

And sometimes I didn't, either.

That morning when I'd gotten to school, I decided I was done eating in the handicapped stall. Okay, so maybe I only made the decision when I got to the vending machine and saw that no one had restocked the cheese crackers I'd polished off on Friday. Knowing that it was pizza day was also a factor: If there was one thing the cafeteria staff at Watkins knew how to make, it was pizza. No way I could make it through math and social studies without getting my hands on at least a slice or four.

Anyway, I'd already faced off with Andres and the rest a couple more times in the hall, and they seemed to have lost interest in me, at least for now. I still waited until about twenty minutes into the period—when all the lines would've died down and most of the popular eighth-graders would've drifted outside to the playground—to head into the hot-food area. I'd grab my food and get out of there fast, no reason to put myself on display any longer than I needed to.

I'd just gotten in line and taken a couple of chocolate milks when I spotted that little kid Jamal and his fat side-kick, whose name I suddenly remembered was Shaun. I was still planning to whup Jamal for laughing at me in the bathroom last week and just hadn't gotten around to it yet.

So I was glaring over at Jamal when his fatass friend Shaun took the last four slices of pizza under the heat lamp. Man, my chest tightened up when I saw that—that's what I get for showing up so late with all the other rejects. Of all the bitches to steal my lunch out from under me!

I was about to step forward when out of nowhere Miss Stipler popped out of the line and tapped Shaun right on the shoulder. The woman who'd come closest to ruining my life had been standing right in front of me, and I hadn't even noticed. She was so small that even Jamal looked big and tough next to her.

"Excuse me, son?" Miss Stipler said to Shaun. "Does your mother know what you're having for lunch today?"

"Nah, I don't think so," Shaun said, looking embarrassed.

"Because right there, what you've got on your tray there, that's more saturated fat than you're supposed to consume in a whole week. If you don't watch yourself, you've got a diabetes diagnosis in your future, do you know that?"

"I'm sorry, ma'am," Shaun mumbled. "I was—well, I was getting all those slices to share with my friend here, ain't that right?" He nudged Jamal in the side, and it took Jamal a second to catch on.

"Oh, yeah, oh, yeah," Jamal said quickly. "Yeah, we always get two each."

"Well, I suppose that's an improvement then," Miss Stipler said. "So I'll let it slide this one time only. But listen, guys, if you ever have any questions about this kind of thing, I run a little informal nutrition clinic out of my classroom during my off-periods. You can bring your parents in, too—good nutrition starts at home, so there's a lot of benefit in you all getting educated together."

I felt a lump rising in my throat, and my skin got very hot. What was going—what was she—was what I thought was happening really happening?

"Hey! What's your problem, boy? I said move it or lose it!"

I nearly jumped out of my skin to see the hairnetted woman behind the counter yelling at me. She was gesturing angrily at the brand-new pepperoni pizza that had just been placed in front of her. "You want some food or you just standing here for the view?"

"Oh," I squeaked out. "Sorry, sorry. Yeah, I'll have . . ." I looked at the pie and then back in front of me. Jamal, Shaun, and Miss Stipler were all moving out toward the lady who swipes everyone's meal cards, and I don't think any of them had even noticed me behind them. "I'll have two slices of the pepperoni, please."

I took the plate she thrust at me, but somehow I wasn't feeling all that hungry anymore. Even the smell made me sick.

I'd been so lost in remembering that afternoon that several minutes had passed in Liz's office in silence. I looked down at my lap. My big, baggy-jeans, fat-kid lap. "What would you've done in my place, Liz?" I asked suddenly.

Liz blinked. She'd been staring at me so intensely it made my skin crawl, like she was in a trance or something. "What do you mean exactly, Butterball, in your place? I believe, as I said, that there's never a time or a place for beating anyone up. Whatever the problem you have with someone, violence is never the answer."

"I get that," I said slowly, and I was really starting

to. "But that's not what I mean. Or not exactly. What's done is done, but now I see—I mean, I understand that nothing really went down the way I thought." I took a deep breath and closed my eyes, then drew my hands to my temples as if to block out the nonexistent glare in that dark-ass room.

I started up again after a long pause. "See, the thing is, I thought Maurice had been telling stories about me. Really bad, nasty stories. Whether those stories had any truth in them is beside the point. Truth doesn't matter so much at Watkins; it's what people say about you that counts, know what I mean? And I was pretty sure that if Maurice kept telling his stories, life as I knew it would be over in a big way. So I did what any decent man would do in the circumstances, and I took the necessary steps to protect myself. You following me?" I said, but I still didn't look up.

I heard Liz make an "mm-hmm" sound and went on, "But now I find out, in the most random possible way, that Maurice never told stories about me to anyone. So when I went over and clocked him on the playground that day, he had no idea what was coming. And all afternoon, I keep replaying the moment over and over, and I see that stunned look on his face, and it doesn't make me mad anymore like it used to. It makes me . . . sad, you know?"

And as I spoke I felt the shaming splash of warm liquid sliding down my cheeks, but I no longer cared all that much what Liz thought about me. Everybody else, yeah, but not Liz, not right then. I was just too tired to give a shit anymore. Tired, and—that word again—really, really sad. "I was wrong, and there's nothing I can do about it anymore."

Liz didn't interrupt to say that of *course* there was something I could do about it, and I was grateful to her for that. We both knew it wasn't true, so what would've been the point? I wasn't playing games, so neither was she. "I mean, Maurice doesn't even go to Watkins anymore, you know? One semester left of junior high and he's gotta start over somewhere else. And the thing is, Maurice was my friend. Yeah, part of the reason was because I didn't have any better choices, but still. He was the only one who ever bothered to be nice to me at that shitty-ass school, and *this* is how I repay him? Man, I'm a bigger piece of shit than I thought."

"You're not a piece of shit, Butterball," Liz said— first time she'd spoken in what felt like an eternity.

"Yeah, I am," I said. "But at least now I know it, right?"

Would my dad still be proud of me if he found out why I did what I did—meaning, no reason at all? Knowing him, probably. But for some reason, that wasn't much consolation. The more I thought about that whole day on the playground, the lower I felt.

A few minutes later, as I pounded down the stairwell outside of Liz's office, I realized that she hadn't asked me, not even once, about the stories Maurice had told about me. Or hadn't told, as it turned out. And that, I decided, was pretty cool of her. She knew when to be nosy and when, as they say, enough was enough.

The apartment really did look nice. Evelyn had listed the cabinet where my mom kept her old TV and the actual TV, too, on craigslist on Saturday night, and she'd sold that shit before we'd woken up on Sunday.

When I got back from Liz's, this young guy and his wife had come by to pick up their purchases, and they'd seemed real excited to be getting such a good deal, never mind that the TV was ten years old and weighed more than most pianos. They paid Evelyn with a stack of twenties, and after I helped the guy lug his loot down four flights of stairs, she peeled one off the top and handed it to me: "my cut," she called it. I wasn't sure what my mom would think of that, but I just nodded thank-you and went right to my Batman box where I stashed my laptop fund.

With the big-ass cabinet out of her way, Evelyn had really gone to town decorating and spent the whole evening rearranging shit till it was just right. She was pretty anal, but by the time she was done, the apartment had never seemed so spacious or comfortable. For a second I thought I might almost have been proud to bring Maurice here. A second after that I felt sick to my stomach again.

There were still half-unpacked boxes stacked all over the place, so I didn't really notice the white box in the middle of Evelyn's glass coffee table. I just pushed it aside with my feet as I kicked them up onto the table.

I reached for the remote, but I guess the Time Warner guy hadn't shown up because when I pressed the power button, only black-and-white static appeared on the screen.

I shut the TV right back off and just sat there, trying to figure out what to say to the woman who was running around our kitchen like she belonged in there. Evelyn worked a more regular shift schedule than my mom, so me and her would probably be spending all sorts of time together from here on out. I wasn't too sure how I felt about that.

After a few minutes, Evelyn walked in with a plate of food in each hand. I saw her glance at my sneakers and the big smudges they were making on her coffee table, but she decided not to say anything. She sat down on the couch next to me and passed a plate over. Then, after thinking about it for a second, she kicked her own feet onto the table, right on the other side of that white box from mine.

"Burton," she began—damn, there she went again! "I wanted to talk to you about something your mom and I've been discussing these past couple of days. Would that be all right with you?"

Instead of answering, I started in on the plate of meatballs she'd brought me. I had to admit they were pretty good. Evelyn was clearly trying to get on my good side, or she wouldn't have cooked a dinner I actually liked. So why couldn't she just let me enjoy the meal in peace?

Evelyn seemed real nervous, probably because she wasn't used to carrying much weight in any conversation. She had that in common with my mom, who she'd just mentioned for the first time. ". . . And Shari wanted me to make it clear that this shouldn't be seen as a bribe or anything like that . . ."

I looked over at Evelyn, who'd been talking on and on. A bribe? A bribe for what?

"And it just so happened that they're updating the data systems at St. Vincent's, and whenever that happens, all the administrative leads are given the opportunity to buy back their old work computers at cost. And well, your mom's always talking about how you want some way to edit your movies, so I offered to . . ."

Evelyn reached forward to the white box that was between us on the coffee table. And all of a sudden I realized what it was, and what exactly she was saying to me.

"It's a couple of years old, but it still works great. And I got the IT guy to wipe the hard drive this morning, so there's a lot of storage space and you can put pretty much any program you want on there . . ."

I threw my plate of meatballs down on the couch next to me and grabbed at the box Evelyn was holding. I'd seen that kinda box before, and I couldn't even believe this was happening. It was a Mac. A Mac laptop, and it was mine. Damn.

"They use Macs at the hospital?" I asked because I wouldn't have expected that of a ghetto place like St. Vincent's, but then what did I know?

Without waiting for an answer, I opened the box and

pulled out the laptop. It was white, not one of those sleek titanium jobs that the DJs use, but still—I would've had to make my bed ten times a day for a year to afford that shit on my own. Man, this was just unreal.

"So I guess you like it?" I heard Evelyn say.

"Oh, yeah, shit, sorry," I said. "Yeah, I love it, for real. Thanks so much."

"No problem at all," Evelyn said, and she almost sounded as happy as I felt. "But remember, it's not a bribe, all right? The timing just happened to work out, and with all the money we'll be saving on rent, paying for it wasn't really a problem. I just thought since you're grounded and all, you'll have some extra time on your hands."

I nodded. Right then I didn't care that I was grounded or who was reminding me of it because I'd rather spend time on this computer than—what? Hang out with the friends I didn't have? Get my face kicked in again?

"Thanks, Evelyn," I said, and if she'd only said my name for the first time the previous day, I don't think I'd ever used hers to her face before, not even once. "Thanks a whole lot."

Someone had vomited in the handicapped stall Tuesday morning, and by lunchtime, no one had bothered cleaning it up, just like no one had bothered to refill the vending machine. There was just no way I was going to sit for an hour smelling that shit. Maybe if I'd had my computer, I could've ignored the stench and gotten down to work, but I'd never bring that laptop within three blocks of Watkins. This school was so ghetto, it'd be jacked before homeroom let out.

So, finally, I decided: Screw it. I'd go back to the cafeteria again, and this time I'd actually eat. I got myself a tray of fish sticks and was just walking toward my old table in the back when Andres slammed right into me. "Oops, sorry about that," he said, but he didn't sound all that sorry. And to prove it, he swiped his hand across my tray and sent a couple of the fish sticks flying.

"Get outta my way," I mumbled under my breath. I was mad, but I wasn't in the mood to start nothing with him. Not now, not ever.

"What'd you say?" Andres asked, real loud, so that everyone who wasn't already staring at us swiveled around to tune in. "Were you crying again, or did you have something you wanted to say to me?"

"Nah," I said. "I just wanna go eat."

"No shit?" Andres said. "But then I guess you don't get a hot body like yours without doing a lot of eating, do you?"

"I guess not," I said and moved to walk around him.

"Ah, I was just kidding, Butterball man. I just wanted to see if you wanted to come sit with us today?" He gestured over to his table where Darrell and Bobbie were sitting and staring right at us. "We haven't seen you around much lately and just wanted to see what was up."

Andres was definitely up to something, and whatever it was couldn't be good. He'd already wasted enough of my time, so I just said "Nah" again and tried to walk around him.

"I'm serious, Butterball, man, me and the boys wanted to rap a little with you. Whatcha doing after school today?"

"I'm busy making movies," I said without thinking and immediately felt stupid. I never talked about that shit, and even if I had, Andres was the last person on earth I would've told. Every day, it seemed like I was giving him another reason to make fun of my ass.

And sure enough, Andres cracked up once he'd processed what I'd said. "Making *movies*, did I hear you right? Movies of what—you eating a fried chicken? Or, I know, how about a whole action sequence that shows you pissing down your leg?"

The kids at the next table laughed their asses off at this, but I felt—nothing at all. It was almost like I was immune. I just left Andres standing there and started walking in a straight line till I reached the back corner table where Maurice and I had sat for so much of seventh grade. When Jamal and Shaun saw me coming, they made a move to get up, but I shook my head and took a seat at the opposite end of the table. I felt them watching me nervously, but I just didn't feel up to getting into it with anyone right then. Instead I started to house what was left of my fish sticks. But somehow, I can't really explain why, they didn't taste half as good as they used to.

The next two days went pretty much the same: I got through them somehow. Just a couple more weeks to go and Watkins would be behind me forever, and you'd better believe I was counting down every single hour.

By that Thursday, my face had healed up almost all the way, and people had gotten bored of checking me out and whispering shit whenever I walked down the hall. It was like I'd gone back to those first months of seventh grade, before I got to know Maurice, when I drifted through my days silent and invisible.

For some reason, though, I no longer minded my

invisibility all that much. Being ignored was a gift, and probably the only reason I'd started to look forward to high school. Most kids at Watkins got fed into Clara Barton High, which was an even bigger school, with students from Roosevelt and Hempstead, too. Maybe it'd be easier to get lost in the crowd again. I was betting on it.

After school on Thursday, I was supposed to head right back to the apartment to wait for the Time Warner guy, who after like a dozen rescheduled appointments was finally supposed to show up to hook up our TV and Internet between four and seven. But it was sunny and warm out, and I'd been cooped up inside all day since I never went out on the playground after lunch anymore. I sorta just wanted to enjoy the sunshine and delay my return to another long afternoon alone in the apartment.

So when school let out at three fifteen, I wandered over to the side door that connected Watkins to Washington Irving Elementary School. It was the same exit Nia and I had taken when we'd walked to OfficeMax what felt like a lifetime ago. I thought I'd go check out what those elementary-school kids were up to—maybe I'd find something to shoot, though that was never all that likely here in Garden City.

I'd just walked out onto Franklin, video camera in

hand, just kinda scoping the scene, when I saw that little kid Malik from the basement of my building. I hadn't known he went to Irving, but I guess it made sense, there not being a whole lot of educational options in this town.

Malik was pretty hard to miss that afternoon. He was standing on the front steps of Irving, hopping from foot to foot, moving up and down the stairs like his sneakers had wings. Freaky as he looked out there, I had to admit the brother was nimble. It really did look like he was flying. For I don't know how long I just stood there, watching my little neighbor move. I'd seen him pull this shit on the stoop sometimes, but this was different: This was right in front of his entire elementary school. And he wasn't embarrassed at all. It was like he didn't care who was watching. Wish I'd been more like that when I was in fourth grade.

A few minutes into Malik's performance, this big guy walked right up to him and started clapping his hands together real loud. "Man, oh, man, you're better than the homeless guy I saw outside the Sunglass Hut last week! Collect any good tips?" he asked in this big booming voice, and a couple of other kids gathered around to watch.

Malik, who'd stopped dancing, shook his head and

backed away from the guy. Damn, he looked scared. Malik was an average-size kid, but next to the guy hassling him, he looked tiny and vulnerable and so sorta crushable.

"I said, you collect any tips, twinkle toes?" the guy repeated even louder, and he was right up in Malik's face now.

Malik kept on shaking his head even as he dug into his pocket and pulled out a couple of wadded-up dollar bills, which the bigger kid snatched right off him.

And before I'd thought about what I was doing, I moved forward until I was standing right between Malik and the guy who'd been bothering him. The guy was big, yeah, but only by elementary-school standards. At Watkins an asshole like him wouldn't last a minute.

"Give him his money back," I heard myself saying. "Now."

The guy didn't move, just shook his head at me. I stared him right in the eyes and read him inside and out. He wasn't nearly as tough as he was pretending to be. I was at least two years older, and I had the weight advantage. And maybe most importantly I had nothing at all to lose.

"Did you hear me?" I said, my voice all low and threatening. "I said give him his money back. *Now.*"

The guy glanced from me to Malik, as if to see if I was kidding. When it became clear that I wasn't, he shrugged and passed the dollar bills back to Malik.

"Good boy," I said. "Now get your ass outta here." Then, before he could make a clean escape, I looked him straight in the eyes again and added, "And don't let me *ever* catch you hassling Malik again, aight? Pick on somebody your own size or I'll make sure you'll regret it."

The guy nodded quickly and then scampered off like I'd just shot at him. About the only thing he hadn't done was wet his pants, not that I of all people could judge him if he had.

Once the guy was gone, Malik looked over at me, as confused as he'd been frightened only a second before. "Thanks," he said. "That was—that was really nice of you."

I shrugged. "You going back to Palace Houses?" I asked. Because that's what the crappy five-story walkup where we lived was called.

"Yeah," Malik said uncertainly. "I guess so."

"All right then," I said. "Let's go."

We hadn't walked five steps toward the sidewalk before I saw her. Nia. She was standing right there, staring at me with those dark eyes.

"Hi, Butterball," she said, and her voice was different than it had been at the 7-Eleven. It was softer, kinder, more like the old Nia from art class.

I must've shown how taken aback I was when I asked, "What're you doing here?"

"Two of my little sisters go to Irving," she said. "I pick them up on the days they don't have dance."

"Oh," I said. "That's cool."

Nia was looking curiously at Malik, as if trying to figure out who he was to me, but I was feeling way too unsteady to get into it right then.

"C'mon, Malik, let's go," I said, and he followed me like a little puppy dog.

About a block past Irving, he said again, "That was really cool what you did back there. I mean it—I really, um, owe you for that."

"Don't worry about it," I said. I already had some ideas of how he could pay me back. "Hey, when we get back to Palace, would you mind showing me some of those moves again?"

"It was all right," I said the next afternoon when Liz had asked me how my week had gone. "I had a cool movie idea yesterday." Now that I had my computer, I was already thinking bigger: I didn't just have to stop with those quickie two-minute videos I shot on the street.

"That's fantastic news, Butterball!" Liz exclaimed. "I'd love to hear about it."

"Well, I wouldn't love to talk about it," I said. But then, realizing how that had sounded, I added, "I mean, I'm just kinda superstitious about that shit. Like talking about it too early might end up cursing the whole project, you know?"

"I understand," Liz said, and she didn't seem offended at all. "If you ever need anyone to sound ideas off, you can always try me out, all right?"

I nodded. "Sure, sounds good."

"And speaking of ideas," Liz said carefully, "I was sort of playing around with one I had about your future."

She waited, and I looked at her, no idea what she was talking about. "Are you about to bump me up to even more sessions a week?" I asked.

"No, actually, Butterball," she said, "I think we'll cancel our Friday appointment and meet again on Monday, and take it on a week-by-week basis from there. What I was actually wondering was if you've ever considered a magnet school for next year."

"A magnet school?" I snorted. "You mean like Bronx Science where all the nerds in Harlem get shipped off to?"

Liz thought about this. "Well, yes and no," she said. "There are other types of magnet schools all over the place, for all sorts of different students—people interested in entering law enforcement, all types of things. The particular one I was thinking of is in Floral Park, for kids interested in careers in the arts."

The woman had my attention, even if I still couldn't figure out why she was telling me all this.

"Now, the deadline for most of these schools has passed," she was saying, "but I do have some pull in the Nassau County school district. So if you were interested in having a look, I might be able to, you know, put in a good word for you."

"But why would you do that?" I asked, more confused than ever. "It's not like I make good grades or anything, especially this past semester when shit's gotten all messed up."

"It's not really about grades at Cunningham," Liz said. "I mean, certainly, grades help, but the bigger emphasis is on creativity. And, you know, creative—direction. Kids who have big dreams and who'd benefit from an environment that supports those dreams."

"But you've never even seen my shit before," I said, more and more baffled by her gibberish. "I mean, you don't even know if I'm any good or not."

"But I do know that you're serious," Liz said, "and at this point, that counts as much, or even more, than anything. I mean, you're in eighth grade, Butterball. No one expects you to be Ingmar Bergman at this point, or even Christopher Nolan."

I raised my eyebrows, surprised old Liz had even heard of Ingmar. I was also kinda flattered she'd remembered what I'd said about Christopher Nolan. Sometimes when I'd sit on that nasty couch rambling on and on, I'd wonder how much Liz was actually absorbing from behind those librarian glasses. In a way, thinking she might be tuning me out the way I tuned out Mrs. Fleming in math sometimes made it easier for me to talk.

And then I thought of something else. "But didn't you say the school was in Floral Park? Isn't that like halfway back to the city? There's no way that'd fly with my mom, especially if she passes all her nursing exams this summer and gets put on an official rotation."

"Yes," Liz said, "Cunningham—the school's official name is the Merce Cunningham High School for the Performing and Visual Arts—is about a forty-five-minute drive from here. But there are trains that go right there, and the school also provides some limited transportation subsidies if they want you enough."

I sighed. There was the problem right there: wanting me enough. Seemed like no one ever did. Liz must've seen the look on my face because she got up off her chair and started moving toward me. I instinctively shrank into the couch, but it turned out Liz didn't have hugging on her mind. She reached out her hand and passed me a stapled-together stack of papers.

"Here," she said, "I've printed out the prospectus and a bunch of application materials. You can have a look over the weekend and talk it over with your mom to see what she thinks. I'm not making any promises, so don't get your hopes up. But I do think Cunningham could be a good opportunity for you. A fresh start might be just what you need."

I looked down at the pages she'd handed me, and my eyes blurred up. *A fresh start:* the exact same words my mom kept repeating the summer after sixth grade, when she'd moved out on my dad without even settling on where we were going next. Yeah, well, look at all the good my last fresh start had done me.

But all I said to Liz was, "Yo, thanks. I'll definitely have a look." Because when it came down to it, I really didn't have much to lose anymore.

I spent the whole weekend just reading that brochure, over and over again. I didn't know public schools like that even existed. The place had a budget and teachers—the brochure kept calling them professors—who were "real leaders in their fields," and they gave kids grants to put on theater productions and dance performances and, yes, even film movies, and they set up internships with real professionals in the city, people I'd actually heard of. The place was unreal.

Now, if only I had a chance in hell of getting in there.

The application was like fourteen pages long, way more detailed than the packets Mom had filled out to get into nursing school. The first night, I filled out all the easy stuff: name, address, Social Security number, that kind of thing. But after that I got stuck.

There were all these questions, page after page of them, that I was supposed to answer "in my own words," whatever that meant. Why did I want to go to Cunningham? Well, two hours earlier I'd never even heard of the place, but now . . . What did I think I'd gain from the experience? Pretty much everything and then some. What were my artistic aspirations? Huh?

But the hardest part of all was the work sample they required all applicants to submit. Still photographs, paintings, a short film . . . Were there really thirteen-year-olds out there who had professional artists' portfolios?

I lay on my bed, staring up at the ceiling, before the idea came to me: Malik. I'd already shot some stuff with my downstairs neighbor, but why not draw it out a little, make a whole movie out of it? I jumped off my bed and went over to my laptop to start mapping it out. First thing the next morning, I was dressed and waiting outside the door of Malik's apartment.

I'd done a lot of shit I wasn't proud of these last couple of months, but I *was* proud of the film I finally managed to pull together as my work sample. I knew as much as I knew anything that it was solid, maybe even good. I called it *The Superhero of Suburbia*, and it was about a quiet, friendless kid who's always struggling to keep his superpower—the ability to fly in broad daylight—a secret. The stuff he did with his superpower wasn't all that heroic, but that was part of the joke: Instead of rescuing babies from burning buildings, S.o.S. would save suburbanites from getting their cars towed and keeping dogs from crapping on perfect lawns.

I used fancy editing tricks to show my downstairs neighbor Malik leaping over sprinkler systems and dancing down mall escalators. And I gotta admit, I'd had a good time working with Malik, who could act as well as he could dance. Maybe when the time came, he'd apply to Cunningham, too.

It'd been Malik's idea to film a bunch of the scenes in Maurice's neighborhood—the big houses there worked a lot better with the plot than the crumbling building where Malik and I lived. All those afternoons we spent in Roydon Oaks, and I'd never run into my old friend, not even once. And that, I'll be honest, was a big relief.

I wasn't looking forward to crossing paths with Maurice again, but I knew exactly what I'd do if it did happen.

I'd walk right up to him, look him straight in the eyes, and say, "I'm sorry." I'm not sure what would happen after that, but it was a start, right?

As for the other kids at Watkins, well, no matter where I went next year, I was pretty much glad to be done with them once and for all. Except for maybe Nia. I'd barely seen her in the last few weeks, but I guess I was the one to blame for that. I'd been so obsessed with getting my movie done—and making sure it was good—that I'd pretty much fallen off the face of the earth. I bought a Kryptonite lock for my locker and spent every free period and lunch holed up in the library, reviewing the footage Malik and I had shot the afternoon before.

About a week before school let out, I came home one afternoon to find my mom sitting on the couch with a big smile on her face. "Let's go out to celebrate when Evelyn gets back in a few minutes," she said. "Should we try Houston's again?"

"Sure, that sounds good," I said, a little taken aback. "But what're we celebrating exactly?"

My mom smiled even wider. "Do we really need an excuse? I don't know, I just . . . Well, you're almost done with junior high, and you've been working so hard on that movie of yours. And I heard from Liz this morning, and she's been very pleased with the progress you've been making. She said that after next Monday's session, you could wind it up for the year, take the summer off."

"She did?" I said. And I'm not sure why, but I wasn't completely flooded with relief the way I'd expected. I mean, all I'd wanted these last few months was for Liz to cut me loose, and now she was doing exactly that—so why wasn't I jumping up and down for joy? For real, what was *wrong* with me?

"Yep," Mom said, "though she said she'll always be around if you ever need some additional sessions. She also mentioned this Cunningham school you've been talking about, honey, and Liz is *very* optimistic. Or, at least, she said she was really pulling for you."

"Well, I gotta turn in my application first," I said. "But I'm almost there; I really am. Hey, hold on, I gotta do something really quick."

I took the cordless phone—another addition from Evelyn's apartment—into my bedroom with me. All of a sudden I was possessed with the urge to call my dad and tell him about my movie and ask him to cross his fingers for my application. I hadn't seen him since the sneakers trip, which was maybe good since I wasn't all the way prepared to answer any questions he might have about what was going down in our Garden City apartment these days.

This Cunningham thing felt big, I thought as I waited for my dad to pick up. It was hard to put it in words exactly. But for once I wasn't just running away from somewhere, which it felt like I'd been doing, in some form or another, these last two years. This time I wanted to go *to* somewhere. And it felt . . . good. Scary, but good.

When I told my dad about the school, there was a }little silence on the other end of the line. "An arts school?" he said. "Say what? That sounds like it's gonna cost me a shitload, and you *know* I ain't trying to hear that."

"No, no," I said, "that's the crazy part. It's a public school. A magnet school, but free like all the others."

"Well, all right then," my dad said, "so long as it's not just some other way for your mom to go digging into my paycheck again."

The music behind him was still blasting real loud, and I knew he had to be at home in his bedroom. The sound system in there was sick.

"You need anything else from me?" my dad asked after a pause.

"No—what do you mean?"

"I mean, why else you call? You been too busy for me these days, so I figured you had to want something out of me."

"Oh, no," I said. "That was it. I just wanted to tell you I was gonna apply, that's all." For some reason I couldn't bring myself to tell him about the movie after all.

"All right, well, if that's really it," Dad said, "then I'd best be getting off the line now if you don't mind. I got a date with destiny tonight, and her name is Angela."

I didn't bother asking him what happened to Diane.

I guess I didn't really care. My dad obviously didn't give a shit about anything I did, so from then on the feeling would be mutual. All of a sudden it stung me hard, the way he'd talked to me, the way he was always talking to me. I'd laid it all on the line about Cunningham, talking to him just like a little kid about how bad I wanted to get in there, and he couldn't even find it in himself to say "Good luck"? Well, screw him then. I was done trying. There were plenty of other places my energy could go.

I hung up and went back into the living room, feeling less than great. All the fizz seemed to have gone out of me. My mom and Evelyn were sitting there dressed and ready to go.

"Oh, I didn't realize you were back," I said to Evelyn, who just nodded in reply to me. She and I still didn't talk all that much, but it wasn't as strained as it used to be.

My mom suggested Houston's again and I wasn't about to disagree, even if my appetite hadn't exactly returned after that phone call. Mom, Evelyn, and I were following the hostess to our booth when my eyes landed right on Nia. She was sitting at the end of a long table surrounded by all her little brothers and sisters.

"Hey!" she called out to me. I had no choice but to stop. I saw no sign of Nia's Aunt Cora, so that was something.

I could tell my mom and Evelyn were curious, so after Nia introduced me around, I stood real still and braced myself. In the most normal voice I had, I said, "Nice to meet everyone. This is my mom, Sheril, and this is her girlfriend, Evelyn. We all came down here to celebrate graduation, I guess just like y'all did."

Nia let out a little gasp. Then she made a sound like "Ah!" as her face broke out into a big smile. Like everything made sense to her all of a sudden.

I shuffled over to her end of the table while our moms and Evelyn made small talk. "So, uh, what're you up to this summer?" I asked Nia.

"Not much," she said. "Just the usual babysitting and hanging out at the Y pool. What about you?"

"Yeah, same," I said. "Nothing big. I'm hoping to work on some movies and, you know, sort through my shit a little."

Nia nodded, but before she could say anything else, I burst out with, "Hey, Nia? Can I say something? I'm sorry I ruined your party, I really am. I don't know what happened. It's just been . . . well, it's just been a really hard year for me is all. But that's no excuse. I shouldn't have done what I did. I'm doing a lot better now, and I'm acting better, too."

Nia smiled at me—she really did have the prettiest smile in the world. "I understand, Butterball," she said. "At least I think I do. And honestly . . . it's okay. If you hadn't been the one to ruin the party, I'm sure someone else would've, you know? That's what my aunt said, anyway, and Cora's usually right about everything. I was really mad, I'm not gonna lie. But . . . I know you didn't mean it deep down."

It felt like this huge weight was lifted off my chest. The leftover anger and misery of that phone call with my dad finally trickled away, probably to return sometime, but not as long as Nia was smiling at me. "All right then, cool," I managed to say. "So it was really good to see you, Nia."

"Yeah, you, too," she said. She paused as if considering something, then added, "And hey, since we're both stuck in town all summer, maybe we could get together sometime if you want. Maybe you could help me babysit one of these days?"

"I'd like that," I said. I couldn't help it; my whole face broke out in the widest grin of my life. "I'd like that a whole lot."

A few minutes later, as I followed my mom and Evelyn over to our booth, I felt almost sick with happiness. Right then I didn't care who knew what about my mom and her relationship anymore.

"I think that girl likes you," my mom whispered as we continued on to our table. She was giggling and seemed a lot younger than usual.

"Ah, shut up, Ma," I said. "She's just nice, that's all. She's like that with everybody. A girl like that, she'd never go for a fat kid like me."

"But Burton," my mom said, "I know you've been too busy to notice, but you're not all that fat anymore."

I looked down at the new pants she'd bought me for the graduation ceremony and shrugged.

"Yeah, well, see if you still say that after all the damage I'm about to do to this menu," I said, and even Evelyn cracked a smile.

"So here it is," I said when I got to Liz's on Monday. On my way over to the couch, I dropped the application packet—complete with DVD—right onto her lap.

Liz looked excited as shit. "You've done it? You've filled everything out?"

"Yep," I said. "It's all good to go now. I worked my ass off on the work sample, but I'm pretty sure I got it right."

"That's wonderful," Liz said. "I can't wait to hand it over."

Liz spent the next few minutes looking over the pages I'd given her. Watching her read my application made me feel a little uncomfortable, like when somebody un-wraps a present you've gotten them in front of you. For some weird reason, I just really wanted Liz to like it.

"I mean, yeah, I did it kinda fast," I said, "but you said I'd already missed the deadline, and I didn't want to let any more time pass, you know?"

Liz was now scanning the pages I'd spent so much time filling out the way somebody reads a half-memo-rized grocery list. "And, like, I know it's not even close to being perfect, but I think I did an okay job, right? I mean, if I didn't, I can always—"

"This all looks just fine to me," Liz said, cutting me off. And then she picked up the DVD I'd handed her. "And this?" she squinted at the label my mom had driven me to the office-supply store to print out. "This is your work sample—*The Superhero of Suburbia*?"

I nodded like I didn't care, but inside I felt shy. "Yep, that's the best I've got. You can watch if you want. It's not dirty or anything like that."

Liz smiled. "I wasn't suggesting that it was. I love the title, and I hope one day you'll let me watch it."

"You can watch it right now if you want," I said. "I mean, not when I'm sitting right here, if you don't mind. That would be a little embarrassing."

"Don't worry, I wouldn't do that to you," Liz said.

There was a silence as we sat there looking at each other.

"So are you sure?" I asked. "I mean, you're sure I should do this?"

"It was my idea, wasn't it?" Liz said. "All right, so I'll be sure to put this in the right people's hands and make a few phone calls, but after that, you're on your own. So *please* try not to screw anything up, okay?"

Liz was chuckling as she said this, but I knew she was dead serious. For as long as she'd known me, all I'd ever done was screw shit up, so it was actually pretty wacked that she was giving me this chance in the first place.

My whole life, school had just been a place where I escaped from whatever was going on at home. Before Watkins, nothing all that bad had ever happened at school, but nothing much good went down, either. It was just—school. Four walls and cheap toilet paper and some bad fluorescent lighting where I passed my time five days a week. Whatever happened with Cunningham, it was kinda . . . eye-opening, I guess, to realize that it could actually be something more.

There was a silence, and I suddenly realized Liz's eyes were drilling into me. "On another subject, you look like you've lost a little weight lately, Butterball. Am I right?"

My mom had said the same thing at the restaurant, and I hadn't known how to respond then, either. "Yeah, well, I've skipped a few meals here and there over the last few weeks," I said. "Just haven't been as hungry as I used to be."

I was now sitting diagonally across from Jamal and Shaun every day. The three of us had never exchanged a word, but it was like we'd called a sort of truce, an agreement not to interfere with one another. It was working for the moment, or at least it sure beat the handicapped stall.

Liz and I spent the next half-hour rapping about nothing in particular—the end of school, how nasty-ass hot it was getting already, our plans for the summer. I'd noticed a neatly zipped suitcase in the corner of Liz's office, right by the mini-fridge.

"Heading out?" I asked, pointing over at it.

"You're very observant, Butterball," Liz said. "Yes, I was—George and I are driving up to Rhode Island for a wedding this weekend, so we're taking the whole rest of the week off and making a vacation out of it. I'm supposed to pick him up at his office at four. Walk me to the car?"

I nodded, and we went back out into the parking

lot together—the first time I'd ever seen Liz outside the confines of her little office. It was bright and sunny out, a different season from when I'd started coming to her at the end of that long dreary winter.

As we passed the fried-chicken place, I stopped and turned to her. "Thanks for helping me out with Cunningham," I said. I wanted to thank her for other stuff, too, but I didn't know how to phrase it exactly. "I mean, I really appreciate it."

"No problem," Liz said. "I think you'd be very happy there, Butterball."

"Yeah, me, too," I said. "Too bad I have more of a chance of getting a pro basketball contract than getting in."

Liz chuckled. "Now, I wouldn't say that. Like I said, I've got friends in high places, and if that DVD's half as good as I think it might be . . ."

"Nah, don't say stuff like that," I said. "I don't want to get my hopes up, you know?"

"It's not the worst thing in the world, is it? Getting your hopes up."

I wasn't sure what Liz meant by that, so I didn't say anything, just started walking across the lot with her again.

"So do you have any plans this summer?" Liz asked as we made our way across the asphalt.

"Nope. Just working on my movies and stuff. My mom wanted me to go to a summer program. But I know she doesn't have the cash for that, and I'm happy working on my own, or with this neighbor kid who starred in that DVD I gave you." I hesitated for a second, then decided to tell her. "But I do have some plans to see that girl I told you about a while back—Nia, remember?"

"I remember *very* well," Liz said.

"Uh, yeah," I said, feeling a little embarrassed. "Well, actually what happened is that I ran into her whole family at Houston's the other night. We all got started talking, and, y'know. Everyone got along real good."

"That's great," Liz said. "Who knows? You could have some summer romance in your future if you play your cards right."

"Aw, c'mon, Liz," I said. "It's not like that at all." And it wasn't, but I couldn't tell her what it was like because I really had no idea. "And another thing I might do—I might . . . Well, I was thinking about stopping over at Maurice's one day, just to say hey and, like, that I'm sorry for everything that happened between us. Do you think that'd be stupid?"

"I don't think that'd be stupid at all," Liz said seriously. "Quite the opposite, in fact. Good luck with that, Butterball—I hope you'll fill me in on how it turns out."

We stopped in front of a beat-up red Honda. Just like I'd suspected, Liz wasn't exactly raking in the big bucks in the therapy business.

"It was good to see you again, Butterball," Liz said now, stooping to unlock her car door. "Stop by anytime you'd like, okay? And remember, if you don't invite me to all your screenings, I'm going to write you a bad-conduct report. Promise you'll keep me in the loop?"

I laughed. "Yeah, yeah, I promise." I hesitated. I felt like I had one last request to make.

"There's . . . just one other thing I wanted to ask you."

Liz turned away from her car to look at me. "Sure, what is it?"

"It sounds kinda weird, I know, but—well, would you mind calling me Burton from now on? Because . . . that's my real name, and that's what I'm going to answer to next year, no matter where I go."

Now it was Liz's turn to laugh. "Of course, Burton. Nothing would please me more. Now have a good weekend, all right?"

"You, too," I said. "Have fun in Rhode Island."

And for a while after she drove off, I just stood there by myself in the parking lot, watching the sun beat down on the asphalt. Then I took a deep breath in and walked back home.